Blood Kin
&
Other Strangers

A Collection of Short Stories & Poems

By
Patsy Evans Pittman

Blood Kin & Other Strangers

© 2008 Patsy Evans Pittman

All Rights Reserved

This book is a work of fiction. The stories and poems contained therein represent an amalgam of experiences, observations and people encountered over the span of a lifetime. Names, characters, places and incidents are products of the author's imagination or are used fictitiously. Any resemblance to actual events or persons, living or dead, is entirely coincidental.

No part of this publication may be reproduced or transmitted in any other form or for any means, electronic or mechanical, including photocopy, recording or any information storage system, without written permission from Publisher Page.

To order additional copies of this book or for book publishing information, or to contact the author:

Publisher Page
PO Box 52
Terra Alta, WV 26764
Tel/Fax: 800-570-5951
www.publisherpage.com

Publisher Page is an imprint of Headline Books

Cover design by Headline Books, based on an early photo of the family of Isaiah S. and Ellen Chipps Dotson, the author's great-grandparents.

ISBN: 0-929915-78-X
ISBN 13: 978-0-929915-78-4

Library of Congress Control Number: 2008923645

Printed in the United States of America

Dedicated to my family
who loves me even when I am unlovable,
celebrates my successes
and lifts me up during my failures

To those dear ones who have gone before
and
those who will come after . . .

In memory of my parents,
Florence H. Ruble Dotson and Berl Dotson
and
my grandparents,
Cora A. Golden Ruble and Clarence E. Ruble

Contents

Waiting For Yesterday 5
In My Father's House 12
Balance Beam 15
Flying Lessons 21
Gardens 25
A Vision Of Violets 31
Sunday Drivers 37
Silent Night, Lonely Night 39
Rose In Winter 44
Aphasia 50
Blood Kin 53
Cousin Joyce's Second Wedding 61
Veronica Lake Jones 67
Another Season 74
Role Model 79
Like A Gift 80
Small Shadows, Silent Dreams 84
Voice Of The Dove 91
After Supper 98
In Mysterious Ways 99
Shadow Of The Mountain 105
The Waiting Room 111
Permission To Leave 119
Important Things—1941 120
The Greatest Danger 121
Crossword 129
The Taste Of Vengeance 133
Always The Mountain 137
Offerings 143
Second Chances 145
Once on a Carousel 149
Blackberry Time 153
What I Learned From Kate 154
A Fine Day To Die 155
All Because Of A Shoe 159

Waiting For Yesterday

Deena stood at the stove in the kitchen of the house where she grew up, giving the creamed tomatoes one last stir. It was hot as blazes, and the window air conditioner in the dining room didn't help much. She blew the fringe of bangs out of her eyes, then swiped at the sweat on her upper lip with the sleeve of her over-sized WVU tee shirt.

Her dad Earl, sitting at the table waiting for his supper, jerked his head toward the window on the far side of the room. "Need a bulb in that there light, Deena. It's been burnt out since yesterday."

Deena didn't quite understand why the electric candles, which her mother had placed in all the windows during the Persian Gulf War, were so important to him. Now, with another war raging in Iraq, she herself couldn't see much sense in it. A million candles, tens of millions of candles, wouldn't bring her husband and all the others back.

Why, Dad? What's the point? she wanted to say. But she didn't. She didn't say it, because in some strange way she *did* understand what he saw in those lights—not young men fighting and dying in some far away country, but a woman, his wife Anna, drying her hands on her apron, humming like she did sometimes, fussing with those candles, moving them a few inches one way or the other, then back where they were in the first place.

Deena stroked the soft fabric of the baggy tee shirt that hung halfway to her knees. *I guess in a way it's like this old shirt of Chris's. Or the bottle of his Aramis shaving lotion I keep by my bed.* Sometimes she would dab a drop or two on her pillow, making believe that he lay beside her.

She turned off the heat under the tomatoes and rummaged in the cabinet for the package of bulbs. As the candle came to life, Earl nodded, tipped his chair back on two legs and hooked his thumbs in his suspenders. "Saw that big ol' bird again this mornin'."

Oh, boy. Here we go again with the great blue herons. When she and her sister Linda were kids, that's all their dad wanted to talk about—the herons that used to nest in the stand of oaks and maples over on the Johnson property. "Ol' Man Johnson, that greedy sonofabitch, might as well'a took a shotgun to 'em when he had that place timbered," he ranted. "Wrecked their nests is what he done." His voice shook with indignation as he went on. "And not only that, them damned mills across the river, pumpin' all that poison in the air . . . And I'll tell you somethin' else—it ain't only the birds they's a-killin'."

Linda, four years older than Deena, would roll her eyes, her mouth curved in a mocking grin. She loved to goad her father, and Earl, red faced and furious, never disappointed her. Half rising, he would lean across the table until they were nose to nose. "Now you listen to me, missy . . . " And just like that, the battle was on.

Now he sat at the kitchen table, arms folded, chin jutting out, primed and ready for an argument. He stared out the window to the creek meandering along the edge of the woods. "I remember when a whole flock a' them nested, raised their little babies, right over there." He swept an arm in a broad arc that encompassed the creek and the reeds and the trees beyond. "Seems like people just can't let things be." He was silent for a few seconds, rocking slightly, then went on. "This one was all by hisself, just standin' there in the shallows, waitin' for his breakfast to swim by, I reckon. Your mother and me, we set out there on the swing and watched him most'a the mornin'."

Deena never knew what to make of it when her dad took on like that. Her mother had died more than a year ago, a year to the day after Chris was killed in Iraq. As for the herons, they disappeared before she was born. It was anybody's guess as to whether her dad's mind had slipped out of gear, or whether he was just trying to get her goat.

Well, she thought, *I'm not about to get into that, not with supper ready to dish up.* Without answering, she split and buttered a hot biscuit, ladled on tomatoes paled to coral with canned milk and more butter, added a generous helping of crisp fried potatoes and set the steaming plate in front of him. No use talking to her dad about healthy eating. He knew what he liked. As she filled her own plate, she thought again that what he liked wasn't doing *her* waistline any good either.

He hadn't touched his food when she sat down and began eating. "Dad, you'd better dig in before your supper gets cold."

He looked at the plate, picked at the potatoes, scooted one extra crisp slice onto the placemat. It lay there, grease seeping into the fabric, distorting the floral print like some weird art form. He poked the biscuit with his fork and growled, "Deena! What the hell do you call this?"

An angry retort stuck in her throat, and she swallowed hard. "I'm sorry, Dad. I know they're not as good as Mom's." *But I try. I really do try.* Anger—at her dad, at the insidious disease that had finally taken her mother, at herself—boiled up as she pictured her mother, sitting there at the opposite end of the table where her dad sat now. Pale and sweating. Stirring, kneading, cutting those damned biscuits with Grandma Perry's antique biscuit cutter.

Earl had barely touched his supper when Deena heard his chair scrape back from the table. "Dad, you surely aren't finished," she said as he shoved his plate away.

He walked to the door, limping slightly with the arthritis that had plagued him lately. "Just leave me be, Deena. Your mother's waitin'." Out in the yard, the swing moved in the evening breeze.

She set his plate down hard, so hard that the leftover potatoes bounced onto the countertop. Angry words sliced through the air before she could stop them. "Dad! She's gone. Mom's dead. And Chris is dead. We have to get over it. Both of us."

"Hell's fire, Deena, you think I don't know that? I *know*." He glared at her for a minute, and she saw a suspicious wetness in his eyes. Then the screen door slammed behind him.

She had wounded him, and she was appalled. How could she have said such a thing? Not knowing what else to do, she began to tidy the kitchen. Scrape the plates. Stack them in the dishwasher. Scrub the countertop. Then she swiped the dishrag over the tabletop, stopping to finger the dents and scratches. *What is it about this old battle-scarred table that brings out the worst in all of us?* She fitted her thumbnail into one deep gouge. Even after all these years, her stomach tightened as she remembered.

That was the evening Linda finally got the nerve to take Jay Johnson's senior ring from around her neck and put it on her finger—

third finger, left hand. She had just turned seventeen. As if to make sure no one missed the huge ring, she tapped the stone again and again on the table. Tap . . . tap . . . tap.

Earl finally took the bait. "Where'd that damned thing come from?"

She told him. "And furthermore," she said, drawing herself up to her full five feet, one and a half inches, "we're getting married."

"The hell you are," he said. "No daughter of mine is gonna get mixed up with that trash."

"Watch me," she said, jumping up so fast that her chair crashed into the wall. She stomped up the stairs to her room and slammed the door so hard that the frosted light globe over the table fell, gouging a deep gash in the table and shattering into a million pieces. Shards of glass sprinkled Anna's green beans like rock salt; icy crystals decorated the sliced tomatoes and fried chicken. Deena sat there, her shoulders hunched, her head bowed, tears creeping down her face. The glass fell around her like rain, and the delectable smell of good food was suddenly overpowering, a suffocating presence in her nose and throat. Her trembling hand reached under the table to pat her father's knee. Why did Linda always have to spoil everything?

Finally, in the thunderous silence that followed, Anna got up and stood behind her husband's chair, draping her arms over his shoulders and pressing her cheek to the top of his head where the wiry red hair was just beginning to thin. "Don't worry, honey," she said. "She's all talk."

Later, when Linda had either sneaked out or was sulking in her room, Anna stood, hands on hips, surveying the damage. Still red-eyed, Deena sidled up to her for a hug.

Anna took her daughter's face in both hands. "It's all right, honey. They're just too much alike, I reckon. Seems like fighting's the only way they know to talk to each other." She scraped Sunday dinner into the garbage, and as she plunged her hands into a sink full of hot soapy water, a chuckle rose with the bubbles. "Your daddy was pushing forty when Linda was born. After so many years, thinking we'd never have babies, I guess Linda was a surprise he never got over." She pulled the wastebasket from under the sink. "Here, Deeney, see if you can clean up some of that glass before somebody gets cut."

Then, still smiling, "By the time you came along, nothing surprised either one of us."

Anna was wrong about one thing, though. Linda wasn't all talk. She and Jay Johnson eloped a few nights later.

Funny how things work out, Deena thought as she ran her fingers over the evidence of that night. It was hard to picture wild, scrappy Linda—the one Earl said would live to regret her marriage—married nearly fifteen years now, with four kids and a minivan. And the way he spoiled those kids, you'd think the whole thing was his idea to start with.

And then there's me. Right back where I started. She looked around the kitchen, at the old-fashioned gas stove, the avocado refrigerator that had to be defrosted at least once a month, the rust and green and brown linoleum that had seen better days. Times like this, she wondered whatever possessed her to sell their house, her and Chris's dream home, nestled at the foot of the Blue Ridge near Charlottesville. That kitchen was bright and modern, with a huge window that overlooked the broad valley and the hazy mountains looming in the distance. That kitchen, with its Amish-crafted oak table, would have embraced a family—the baby in a high chair, two, maybe three older kids—giggling and chattering over dinner while she and Chris basked in the Norman Rockwell scene.

Then, overnight, the world changed. Their sheltered life cracked as the Twin Towers crumbled. They clasped hands as the horror spilled from the TV screen into their cozy den, courtesy of CNN. Like a movie they could choose to watch or not, the images of death and destruction continued: the hunt for bin Laden, Afghanistan bombed, Afghanistan invaded, bombs over Baghdad. Shock and Awe. And yet, there in their mountain fortress, thousands of miles away from the bloodshed, they felt safe. They didn't believe—couldn't believe—that Chris's Marine Reserve unit would be called up. But it was.

Within weeks, when the froth of pink blossoms on the weeping cherry tree in the front yard swept the blue sky of a perfect spring day, two spit-and-polish, dress-uniformed officers knocked on the door of the house huddled in the shadow of the Blue Ridge. As their words eddied around her, Deena watched petals swirl from the tree to the ground, and knew that not even the mighty mountains could protect her.

She remembered little of that year, and now, when she thought of it at all, remembered only the fog that hung in the meadows until midday, the clouds, impaled on the mountain peaks, writhing, breaking free, melding with the fog, suffocating her like a gray blanket.

When her mother died a year later, Deena packed the car with everything that mattered. Then she closed and locked the door of the house at the foot of the mountains, leaving behind the ghost of the man who would never father their unborn children. Somewhere between Harrisonburg and the West Virginia border, the fog began to clear.

Now, standing at the sink in the 1950's kitchen, Deena watched her dad there in the old swing, his arm stretched along the rough wooden back, his face turned toward the vacant space he embraced, as if the love of his life really were seated there. *Oh, God, he looks so lonely.* She remembered how, on the day she came home to New Martinsville, he stroked her hair, his rough hands catching the fine strands, how she cried in his arms as they both grieved for what they had lost.

She dried her hands, opened the door and went out, down the steps. Earl looked up but didn't say anything. The chains creaked under her weight as she sat down next to the ghost of her mother. A soft breeze lifted her hair, drying the sweat on her neck. The fragrance of new-mown grass blended with the almost too sweet scent of honeysuckle and multiflora rose. Fireflies shimmered over the lawn like earthbound stars, and cicadas began their raspy song.

She looked back at the house glowing with soft light, the house where she had lived most of her life, a candle burning in every window. She leaned her head back and closed her eyes. Joined by the gentle motion of the swing, they sat in silence.

When Earl finally spoke, his voice was so soft she thought at first it was her imagination. "I *know* she's gone," he said. "But sometimes I have to pretend, just to make it through another day. Sometimes, I know it's nothin' but wishful thinkin', but it's like if I try hard enough, she really will come back."

Unable to face the pain in his voice, feeling its echo in her own heart, she kept her eyes closed. Minutes passed. Then, in the silence, she felt a light touch on her hand.

"Look," he whispered.

There, rising from the creek with the gathering mist, she saw it—a great blue heron, huge and graceful and magnificent, its powerful wings thrusting into the evening sky. It did not circle or drift on the air currents like lesser birds, but, long legs trailing like a banner, its measured strokes carried it straight for home—straight for the second growth forest on what was once the Johnson farm. Within seconds it was only a dark silhouette.

Remembering the stories, his obsession with this creature, she reached for her father's hand just as he reached for hers. Bound by the tenuous thread of awe and the tangled web of ten thousand yesterdays, they watched until the great bird disappeared in the fading light.

In My Father's House

This house,
this house is old—
almost as old as he is, I guess.
The floors creak
as if remembering footsteps
of children grown,
a wife long gone,
as if remembering the scrape
of chairs after Sunday dinner.

This house,
my father's house,
sighs and settles in the chill of night,
cries for the son,
the son flawed at birth, dead at sixteen,
the wife, the stay-at-home mom,
who tried to build a life
on recipes and romances and soaps
and never quite succeeded.

This house,
this lonely old house
expands in the heat of day,
speaks a language all its own,
tells of the father,
handsome in navy blue,
called to war, leaving three daughters—
tomboy and poet and rebel—
and the son he hardly knew.

And when finally he returned,
with gray in his hair
and a bellyful of strange, exotic places,
no desire to ever leave,
he gardened and gambled and drank,
and sweated eight, ten, twelve hours a day
at the fiery furnace of the steel mill
for love of the tomboy and the poet and the rebel
and the son he hardly knew.

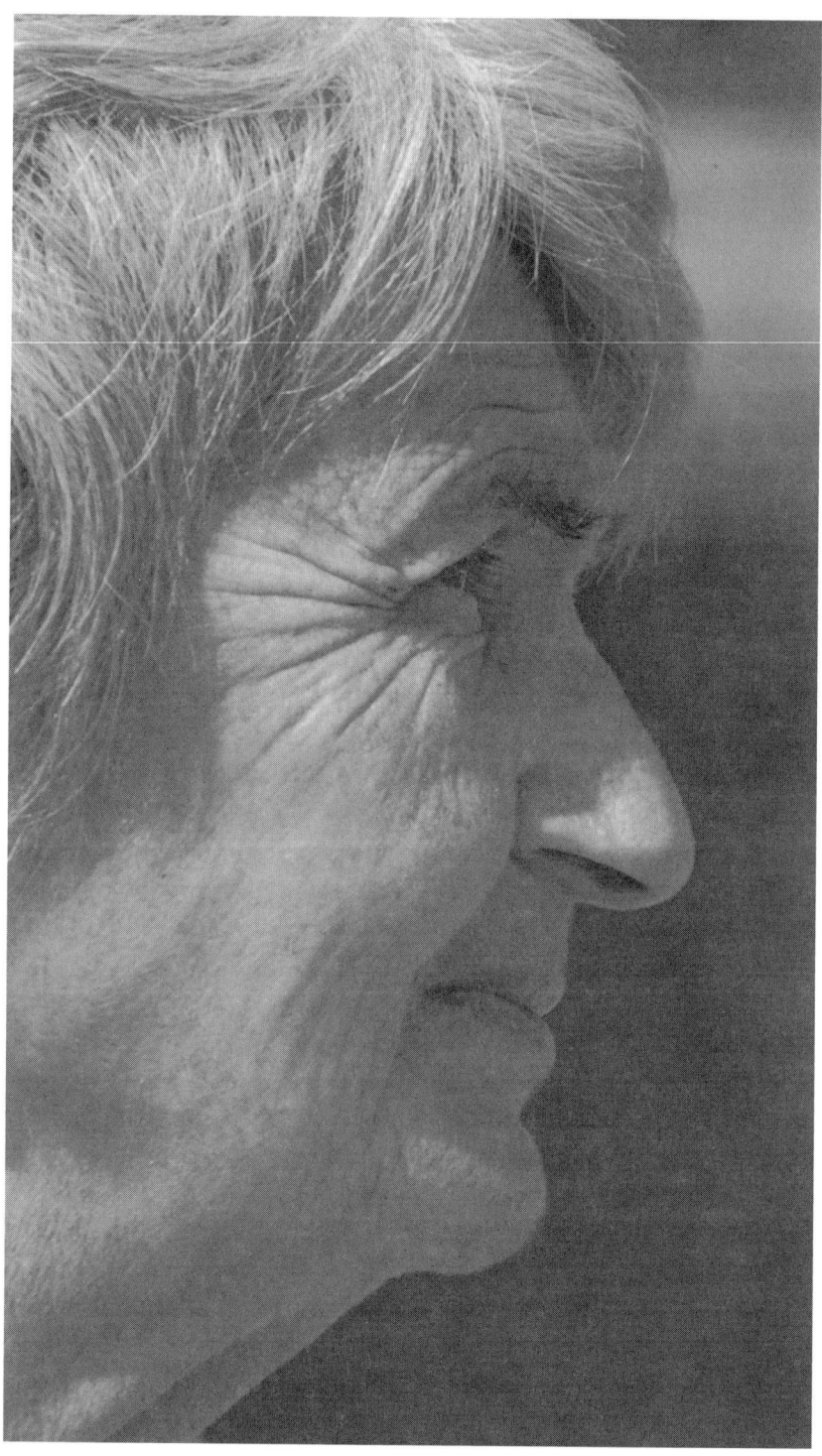

Balance Beam

Oh, Momma, I whisper. *Where are you?* Her fingers scuttle across the coarse cotton sheets like fiddler crabs roused from their burrows. Her eyes, wide and frightened, focus on the door.

"Where's Mary Rose?" she asks in a fretful voice that doesn't sound at all like my mother. "She should be home from school by now. Where's Mary Rose?"

"Don't worry about Mary Rose, Momma. She's fine." It would have done no good to tell her that my younger sister was long past school age, married to a doctor and living in Atlanta. I can't tell her, either, that Mary Rose has been within seventy miles of Ferndell twice in the last six months and hasn't come near "the hospital," as she calls it. *CareHaven isn't a hospital,* I want to scream. *It's a place where people go to die!*

Safe in her sanctuary five hundred miles away, Mary Rose calls a couple of times a month. "I don't know how you *stand* it," she always says in that honeyed southern accent she acquired, along with her three-carat diamond ring, when she became engaged to *The Doctor,* as she refers to him. "And *really* now, Maggie dear, do you *really* need to go over there every day?"

Well, yes, sister dear, I do need to go every day. Really. This isn't one of your fancy personal care homes—it's a nursing home, and not the best in the world at that. I need to see that she's being cared for. I need to feed her dinner. Who's going to see that she eats if I don't? Do you really think the staff has that kind of time? But most of all, she needs to know that she's not forgotten.

"Now I myself can't *stand* it when she cries. When she begs me to take her home . . . Oh, it just breaks my *heart!*"

Well, get over it, sister, because that's how it is. That's how it's going to be—worse and worse and worse—until she dies.

I cover the icy hands, translucent as onionskin, with my own, partly to warm them, partly to calm their frantic searching. "I love you, Momma," I whisper.

Her face lights up, and she withdraws one hand to caress my cheek. "Mary Rose, sweetheart. I knew you'd come."

"It's me, Momma. Margaret," I say through the tightness in my throat. I move closer so she can see me. "It's Maggie."

She looks at me and the light dies. Then she turns her face toward the wall.

The long hard day settles on me. They're all hard, it seems—today no worse than the one before, and all the ones sure to come after. I'm bone weary. My head aches. My back aches. My feet, even in the sensible pumps, feel as if they're on fire.

I want—oh, how I want—to sleep, to feel the sun on my face, the breeze tangling my hair, to sit down to a meal that doesn't come from a can or a box. I want a job with a future, instead of the dead-end temporary assignments that give me the time to spend with Momma and my daughter Hannah. Most of all, I want someone to take care of *me. Me.* I've never known, or can't remember, what that's like.

Suddenly, Momma grabs the bed rails and tries to sit up. "William?" she calls, looking toward the door. "William! I'm in here." She cocks her head, listens for a few seconds, then, pointing at me, "Go get your daddy! He's come to take me home."

Gently I try to press the frail body back against the pillows. "Who are you?" she demands. "Get away from me." Then, louder, "William!"

I've exhausted all the kind lies—*Daddy's at work. Daddy's busy. Daddy can't come right now.* And still she watches and waits. Finally, I say it. "Momma . . . he's dead. Daddy's dead."

The fragile hand draws back and strikes my cheek with surprising force. "Liar!" she screams. "Liar! Get out! Get out of here!" Her screams escalate with every breath. "Help me! Oh, please, somebody help me! She's trying to kill me!"

Finally, a nurse strolls in, strolls back out, and returns with a sedative. By the time Momma falls asleep, eyes closed and mouth open, I realize Hannah's gymnastic meet is already underway.

It's still early, and there is almost no traffic. David, my ex-husband, always said this was a one-horse town, and I guess he was right. I like it that way, but he hated small town life, hated the job that kept him here, and finally, I think, hated me. He couldn't wait to get back to the big city bright lights, and when he finally left, I felt more relief than grief.

The gym is a big old barn of a building, drafty and none too clean. I pick my way across the graveled parking lot and push open the metal door to the smell of sweat and chalk and leather. There is a spate of polite applause as a child no bigger than a cricket finishes her floor exercise and back-flips across the floor. That's the event where Hannah really shines, but I've already missed her performance.

The crowd is sparse, and there are plenty of seats, but I stand at the railing for a moment watching Amanda Braden, an enchanting gnome of a child. She flips and flies and floats through her routine on the balance beam, supremely confident, apparently unconcerned that her landing site is only a little wider than the palm of my hand.

And then there's Hannah. As always, after being away from her for a few hours, my breath catches at the sight of her perfection—the creamy skin, the mass of dark red curls. How, I wonder, could such an awesome creature come from such a miserable union?

She chalks her hands, then her feet. At almost thirteen, her body in the teal and navy leotard is still as slim and flat as a child's. She has apparently done her hair herself, and it hangs down her back in a fat messy rope, curls sticking out every which way. I usually help her put it up in a tight braid for gymnastics, but today—well, today I wasn't there. That seems to happen a lot lately.

She stands at the edge of the mat, drawing into herself, disappearing into a world so contained that there is only room for her and that narrow plank. "Focus, Mom. It's all about focus," she has told me again and again. I knew she was parroting her coach.

She vaults onto the beam. With my fear of heights, it seems a long way off the floor. She dances along the beam in dainty little ballet steps; she leaps and dips and turns in mid-air. She is incredible. Then, poised, she raises her arms, and my stomach clenches. She's going to do what I had begged her not to. A double back handspring.

She has practiced for weeks, even marked an area the size of the beam with tape on her bedroom floor. Long after she should have been asleep, I could hear the solid thump thump thump as she landed again and again and again. She begged me to let her go to the gym before school, after school, weekends. There's no stopping Hannah when she decides to do something. "Don't worry, Mom," she said this morning when I dropped her off at school. "I'll nail it. Just watch me."

But as she completes the first flip, a thick curl escapes from the braid and whips into her face. *Focus, Mom. It's all about focus.* Horrified, I see her foot slip, her hand miss. I hear a sickening *thunk* as the end of the beam catches her temple.

The stunned silence echoes like a gong in my head. Hands reach out to help me as I squeeze through the railing; they propel me toward the crumpled form lying so still on the blue mat. I feel as though I'm slogging through deep water. Will I never reach her?

Finally—finally, I kneel beside her, touch the cool, pale cheek, smooth the hair from her forehead. Shout silent hallelujahs as she opens her eyes and struggles to sit up.

"It's okay, baby," I whisper. "Just lie still."

Her coach checks her pulse and signals for a stretcher.

I stand by, helpless, as she is loaded into the ambulance. It screams through the early winter darkness, and I follow. By the time I screech to a stop at the Emergency Room entrance, she is being wheeled in the door, and I follow to Trauma Room #3.

The sickly green curtain billows as doctors and nurses bring their machines, and I pray, their healing. I'm unaware of my tiredness, unaware of time. I hear moans from the next room and am unmoved. I know only—I care only—that my child is hurt.

I'm to blame; I know that. I should have insisted she get her hair cut. *Oh, my God, will they have to shave her head?* And where was I when my baby was struggling with those beautiful, wild curls? I was with my own mother, trying to make her remember that she has *two* daughters—and only one is named Mary Rose.

The long evening straggles into night and then on to the first hours of the new day. I hold my breath as a young doctor—too young to trust with my baby's life—pulls back the curtain and squats down beside me.

"She has a concussion, but she'll be fine in a couple of days," he says. "One thing for sure, she won't be doing her flying trapeze act for a while." I sag back into the chair, and he pats my shoulder. "We'll keep her overnight, just to make sure everything's okay."

The room is quiet and dim. Hannah lies against the white pillow like a porcelain doll; long lashes flutter as she struggles to stay awake. An ugly purple bruise spreads from her left temple and circles her eye. Nurses come and go, monitoring her vital signs, shining a light into her eyes to check the dilation of her pupils. She moans, raises her arms as if trying to complete her routine.

My fingers worry the stiff hospital sheets that shroud the tiny body. Exhausted, I settle back into the battered recliner, surrounded by the hospital smells and sounds—the odor of illness and antiseptic, the squeak of rubber soles on tile, doors opening, doors closing. Voices hushed, voices urgent. My cell phone chirps, and I dive for my purse, not wanting to disturb Hannah, who is finally quiet, yet not wanting to answer, for I know that only bad news comes calling at this hour of the night.

"Maggie, honey, it's Vernie," a rich Southern voice says. Even as I steel myself for the latest crisis, a corner of my mind wonders at the quick intimacy that has developed between this plain woman with the glamorous name and me. But then again, why not? Veronica Lake Jones is my mother's champion when I'm absent. Her surrogate daughter.

"Now don't you get yourself all worked up, Maggie. Your mamma's just having an episode. Can you come?"

An episode. Well, I guess they have to call it something. Still, that seems like such an ordinary word for the occasional wildness that possesses my mother—the terror, the iron determination to escape the confines of her bed, the incredible physical strength.

"Yes, of course. I'll be right there, Vernie."

I kiss my daughter's cool, pale cheek, caress the tumble of curls and tiptoe from the room.

I stop at the desk to be sure they have my cell phone number, then push open the door into the cold, clear, star-spattered night. It is like stepping into another world, but my same old car is parked exactly where I left it, and it starts with the same reluctant errrrrrr.

The streets now are completely deserted, and it only intensifies the feeling of stepping into a parallel universe.

A few battered cars, the kind driven by the minimum wage heroes who keep places like CareHaven running, are scattered at the far end of the parking lot. My footsteps echo in the empty corridors, but as soon as I round the corner to my mother's room, I hear her heavy breathing, her guttural growls. Two husky male aides and a doctor are positioned around her bed. Her eyes shift this way and that, slyly searching for a way around or through them. Perceiving a weakness in the wall of flesh, she lunges for an opening, only to be blocked once again. Vernie stands at the head of the bed, crooning softly, trying to banish the darkness that has claimed my mother.

The doctor eyes me, makes no attempt to hide his hostility. "This wouldn't happen if you would allow us to restrain her," he says.

Tether my mother to the bed like an animal? Tie her up like a dog? "That's not going to happen," I say through clenched teeth as I elbow him aside.

I smile and stroke my mother's hand. Keeping my voice light, I say, "Momma, I'm surprised at you—all these men in your room at this hour! What will the neighbors think?" She looks at me, and I can see her struggling to make her way back from that faraway place. As she begins to relax, the men fade from the room. Vernie stands for some minutes, her hand on my shoulder. Then she too leaves, and we are alone.

I pull a chair up to the bed and stroke the cold hands, spotted and frail, the wrinkled forehead. Softly I hum the same lullaby I sang to Hannah—the same one Momma had sung to me. At long last, she sleeps, her hand gripping mine, her breathing slow and shallow, a gentle snuffling in the quiet room.

I rest my head on the cool metal rail as the events of the long day wash over me, wave after wave. "Oh, Momma, I'm so tired." Now the tears come, hot and uncontrolled.

And as I sob, a gentle hand smoothes my hair. Faintly, ever so faintly, a tentative voice echoes my lullaby. Then I hear my mother whisper, "Hush, Maggie. Maggie, don't cry."

Flying Lessons

He sits at the table, head down, stirring his mashed potatoes and green beans into a disgusting mess. My son Donnie, with the wild red hair and ears like doors left ajar, is at it again. I look at him, and for an instant, I see Del. I see Donnie's father, and a shiver crawls up my arms.

"Stop it!" I hiss through clenched teeth. My hands, too, are clenched. Sometimes I read those horror stories of child abuse and wonder if maybe I have that kind of evil in me.

He tugs at his hair and looks up, not quite meeting my eyes, but I frown anyway.

"You're gross," Kara says, kicking his chair. "Gross and dumb. Dumb Dummy Donnie."

"Kara, leave your brother alone," I say, but I'm thinking, *God, she's a cute little rascal.* She grins at me and gets in one final kick.

Kara was the easy one—easy pregnancy, easy birth. A beautiful baby. She's five now, pretty as a picture. Petite, with hair to her waist, straight and blond.

Donnie, on the other hand, has been a problem from the minute he was born—no, from the minute that slippery little fish swam upstream and found its target. Ten minutes later, I swear, I was sick, and I stayed that way for nine hellish months. Donnie was not a pretty baby. I may as well say it—he was ugly. Fat and ugly, like a little red Buddha. And cry? He cried all the time.

"Can't you shut that damned kid up?" Del would yell. I tried everything—walking, rocking, feeding, changing. I couldn't make him stop.

I was accident prone in those days. Fell down a lot, ran into things. Always had a black eye or bruises. I dropped everything I picked up, burned stuff that shouldn't even have been on the stove.

With Donnie crying all the time, I just couldn't seem to get it right. And Del never was a patient man. He expected to get what he wanted when he wanted it, whether that happened to be supper or sex.

The day he left with another woman was the day my prayers were answered. It was like God suddenly realized I was down here, hurting, needing. Within six months, I met John, and before long, we were married and had Kara. He's a good man, John is, good to me, and good to Donnie. It's John who works overtime to pay for all the extras Donnie needs.

I get up to clear the table, and Donnie carries his plate to the sink. "I'm sssorry, Mommy," he says, still not looking at me. He rubs against me like a dog wanting to be petted, but I move away.

"Just get busy on that homework. You're going to fool around and get kept back again." My voice is sharper than intended, but there are times I can hardly stand to look at him. His teacher has hinted Donnie's not real bright, and maybe she's right, but he doesn't try. He doesn't even try.

He sits at the table, one hand tangled in his hair. Del used to do that. His math book is open, but he's staring out the window, watching the birds at the feeder John helped him build. If only he'd pay as much attention to his lessons as he does to those damned birds.

"Donnie..." I warn.

The next time I look, he's drawing birds in the margins of his paper. They look real enough to sing, but as Miss Thomas wrote on last week's assignment, in big red letters, *THIS ISN'T ART CLASS!!* It just rolls off. He doesn't care.

Kara twirls around the kitchen. She's dying to take ballet lessons, but there's no money. It goes for Donnie's speech therapy and glasses and tutor. John insists on that; you'd think he was Donnie's father instead of Kara's. I'm too hard on Donnie, he says.

Kara spins into me, and dishwater sloshes onto the floor. "Honey, why don't you go upstairs and play."

She pouts and whines, but finally stomps up the stairs.

I hear the basketball bouncing on the driveway and know Donnie has sneaked out. Oh, to hell with it, I think. Let him go.

As I finish the supper dishes, there's a thud against the picture window, and I brace for the sound of breaking glass. But it's not a ball that bounces away; it's a bird. Stupid things. They're always flying into that window, making a mess, leaving feathery prints on the glass.

I ease the sliding door open and step into a spring evening laced with the scent of lilacs and a fragrance I can't name. The bird, a scrap of gray velvet against the green grass, lies very still. Donnie kneels, strokes the tiny body, traces with one finger the bright yellow band across the tail.

Like scenes from a video, images flash through my mind. A lump of gray fur. A helpless kitten, lying so very still. My Stormy. I hear Del laughing. *I told you to keep that damned cat away from me, didn't I?* I catch my breath at the painful clarity of it.

Donnie holds the bird tenderly. "Poor little birdie," he whispers without a trace of his usual stutter. "See, Mommy? It's just a little bit hurt."

It's a cedar waxwing, a young one. I remember how flocks of them stripped the berries from my mother's holly bushes. The head lolls to one side, and I touch the downy feathers. "It's dead, Donnie," I say as gently as I can.

He cradles the limp body in both hands, holds it close to his face, then tosses it into the air. Catches it and tosses it once more, but this bird will never fly again.

"Mmmmake it fffly, Mommy. Please make it fly." He looks at me, pleading, eyes large and luminous behind his glasses.

I look back, look into my son's eyes, until finally, I see him. Not Del. Not Kara. I see Donnie.

He lays the bird on the ground, wipes his hands on his shorts and swats at the wetness on my face. "Don't cry, Mommy. It's just a stupid ol' bird. See?" He nudges it with his foot. "Just a stupid ol' bird."

My hand smoothes the tangled hair. His arms are around my neck, and this time I don't pull away.

Gardens

Marie popped the last bite of coffee cake into her mouth, licked her fingers and waited. Her sister-in-law Ruth stood at the sink, viciously scrubbing a skillet that should have been clean several minutes earlier. Finally, when the silence was stretched to its limit, Marie said, "Okay, Ruth, spill it. What's the trouble?"

Ruth's shoulders slumped as she turned from the sink. "I swear, Marie, sometimes I think there ain't nothin' in this world but trouble and worry." She wiped her hands, then her eyes, on her apron and sat down at the table.

"Talbot still messin' with that woman downtown?"

"Yeah, but it ain't that. I reckon the trouble I got now is about as bad as it gets." Ruth straightened the salt and peppershakers, wiped a coffee ring from the red and white oilcloth. She looked at Marie, then away. "It's Angie."

"Angie? Ruth, I tell ya, you gotta quit pushin' that girl so hard. She's a good kid. Why, I'd get down on my knees and thank God for one like her after what I went through with my Clarissa."

"She's pregnant. I reckon maybe two months gone."

Marie's head dropped forward and her plump body seemed to shrink. "Oh, God, no. Not Angie."

It was no secret that Marie thought Angela Jarvis could walk on water. Talbot was nowhere to be found that November morning when Ruth went into labor with Angie, and the nearest hospital was almost an hour away.

"Marie, for God's sake, get over here quick!" Ruth had gasped into the phone.

Marie found her on the floor, writhing in pain, while little Jimmy, still in diapers, cried in his crib. As the day wore on, Ruth's screams faded to weak moans, and Marie, desperate, finally took matters into her own hands. Sweating and cussing, she found one tiny foot, then the other. She could feel Ruth's flesh tear as she pried and pulled and tugged, but she figured that was better than doing nothing and letting them both die. She was nearly convinced that was going to happen anyway when the slippery bundle, arms upraised, finally popped out like the cork from a jug of cider gone bad.

Marie couldn't explain it, but there was something special, something real good, between her and Angie. She loved her own daughter. God knows she did, even when Clarissa seemed bent on making that as tough as possible. But it was different with Angie. How could you *not* love her? So pretty and sweet. Always laughing and singing. Never still a minute. "For heavens sake, Angie, will you light somewhere?" Ruth would say. But even when sitting perfectly still, she seemed to be moving. Oh, yes, you knew when Angie was around. And smart! Why, that girl could do anything she wanted.

Without thinking, Marie stirred another spoon of sugar into her coffee and picked at the cake crumbs left on the plate. "The Johnson boy, I suppose?"

"Of course, 'the Johnson boy.' Didja think she picked somebody up off a' the street?"

"Ruth, you know I didn't mean that." Marie paused, wondering what to do, what to say next. "So what's she gonna do?"

"What's she gonna do? She's gonna get married; that's what she's gonna do."

"But she's only fifteen-years-old. My God, Ruth, she can't get married at fifteen. She won't have a chance, and neither will the baby. She's smart. She's gotta finish school. I always thought she might even go to college. Be somebody, not like you and me. Besides, I never did like that boy. Sneaky. Always was sneaky, even as a little kid."

"She's fifteen-years-old, jus' like I was, and she's gonna get married, jus' like I did." The lines around Ruth's mouth deepened. "Had me two babies and buried one of 'em, my sweet little Jimmy, all before I was eighteen. And now, jus' look at me. I got all this." Her laugh was harsh as she opened her palms to the cluttered kitchen, the cracked linoleum and soot-streaked walls. "Live like a queen, I do."

Marie thought a long time before she spoke again. "Is this whatcha want for Angie? Is this whatcha really want?" Then, lowering her voice and her eyes, she went on. "Not every seed that gets planted sprouts, ya know."

Ruth jumped up so abruptly that Marie cringed. "Is that your answer? Murder it? I swear to you, Marie, if you even breathe such a thing to Angie, you'll never set foot in this house again. And if you think I don't mean it, just you try me." She leaned over the table until she was nearly nose-to-nose with the other woman; then, remembering, knowing Marie remembered, she wilted into her chair.

The morning was nearly gone when Marie finally said goodbye and began the quarter-mile walk to her house. It was April, warm, and the graveled road, rutted and muddy from the winter snows, was bordered with new growth. Wild azaleas just beginning to bloom clung to the rocky cliff that rose like a wall on one side, and on the other, at the bottom of a deep ravine, Big Gully Creek, swollen with the spring run-off, roared over the rocks. The highfalutin ladies from Camden and beyond who claimed Marie Jarvis as their personal seamstress would have said it was "Magnificent! Just magnificent!"

Most times, Marie thought so, too, and she sometimes wished she dared use that word. *Magnificent.* But today she hardly noticed. She was thinking about Angie, poor kid. Probably scared to death, not knowing which way to turn. She could just imagine the scene when Ruth first found out. They weren't what you would call real close, Ruth and Angie. Seemed like when she lost Jimmy, Ruth sort of pulled back from Angie too.

The door to Marie's cottage was unlocked as it usually was, and as she stepped inside to the quiet, the neat, spare furnishings, she drew a deep breath, the first full breath she had drawn since the awful news. She would do anything for Angie, always had, but this—there was nothing she *could* do. That was the awful part. There was nothing she could do.

In her bedroom, a simple white dress with delicate flowers embroidered on the skirt, basted and ready to be fitted, hung over the closet door. She had spent hours on it, a surprise for Angie's graduation from junior high. Was it now to be her wedding dress?

The pain was so sudden and so real that she had to sit down on the bed, but that was a mistake, because there on the stand was Angie's picture. She was four maybe, no more than five, all eyes and freckles, and under the glass were five once shiny pennies. They had been warm and damp when the child pressed them into her hand.

"They're for you, Aunt Marie. To buy a car, so you won't have to walk when you come to see me."

"But I can't drive," Marie answered.

"That's okay. I'm almost big. I can drive you." Angie bobbed her head so hard that light brown hair, bleached nearly blond by the sun, swung into her face.

Marie looked at the picture a long time. *Ah, Angie,* she thought as she heaved herself from the bed, *you haven't changed, sweet innocent lamb. Don'tcha know there's a few things you just ain't ready for? Don'tcha know there's always them that'll take advantage?* She sighed and shook her head. *Ya gotta be careful, honey. Ya gotta be real careful.*

Finally, she dried her eyes and blew her nose and went into the kitchen to clean up the dishes from the cake she had baked that morning. Finding a crust stuck to the pan, she scraped it out and stood at the kitchen window, eating but not tasting. The grass was greening in patches, and she watched as cloud shadows moved across the garden that Hank had laid out. It was empty now. Come summer, it would still be empty. The soil was so sandy, so poor, that not even weeds thrived there.

Leaning a little to the left she could see the broad strip of rich loam, forty or fifty feet wide, that bordered the woods, but a garden there would have meant grubbing out roots, spading and hoeing, and ol' Hank, the lazy dog, wasn't about to let himself in for that much hard work.

Brushing the crumbs into the sink with the side of her hand, she marveled again at the unexpected blessing of the mining accident. She knew it was awful to be glad Hank was dead, but she was. He had been stupid and arrogant and lazy. A tomcat, just like Talbot. All the Jarvis men were, even the old man. Fat and ugly as she was, old man Jarvis had tried to get her into a corner more than once.

Now she had this little house, and the money she made from her sewing. The ladies from town, who brought their store-bought clothes for altering, now brought their daughters' giggling bridesmaids and yards and yards of pale material for their pale puffy dresses, then a little later, soft batiste and satin and lace for christening gowns.

It was enough, more than she had ever hoped for. Marie Jarvis might not be much good for anything else, but put a needle, any kind of needle, in her hands, and her pudgy fingers took on a life of their own. It was a gift, she supposed.

The yellow school bus stopped at the forks of the road, and Angie, head down, arms loaded with books, got off. Minutes later she stood in Marie's kitchen, pale and dark-eyed, looking tinier than ever.

"Mama told you, didn't she?"

Marie opened her arms, and the girl barreled into her.

"Oh, Aunt Marie, I was so stupid! Daddy will just kill me. Can't you do something, Aunt Marie? Please?"

The drip drip drip of the faucet marked time as the years rolled backward, and it was Ruth's voice she heard pleading, "Help me, Marie. Please!"

Marie had the eerie feeling that time was, after all, just a movie that played over and over. Never a chance to put right what went wrong, just the same plot, over and over and over again.

She had been sitting on the couch that day, knitting a tiny pink sweater for the infant Angie. Ruth came in without knocking, just as she always did. She carried Angie, and Jimmy, not yet two, was wrapped around her knees. She was crying. "Marie, you've got to help me. Oh, please, help me! If I have another baby Talbot will just go crazy. I swear, I'll kill myself—if he doesn't kill me first. Please, before he finds out."

Finally, Marie, unable to bear it any longer, slipped the rows of pink yarn onto one needle and carried the other into the kitchen. Angie, fast asleep, sucked on a chubby fist. Marie laid her on the bed, and sent six-year-old Clarissa and little Jimmy to the store for ice cream.

Two months later, Jimmy died of pneumonia. At the funeral, Ruth, dry-eyed, looked at Marie and said in a flat voice, "It's our fault, you know. God took him because of what we did. You watch. He'll take your Clarissa too."

And in a way, she was right. Clarissa left home the day after her eighteenth birthday, and Marie had heard from her exactly four times since. Three post cards and a telephone call, each time asking for money.

Now Marie stepped back, wiped the girl's wet cheeks with her fingers. "Angie, have you been to the doctor?"

The girl shook her head. "No—I just used one of those kits from the drug store."

"Sometimes they're wrong, honey." She took the sweet young face in her hands. "Maybe it's a mistake. Maybe you never was pregnant. Angie, do you understand what I'm sayin'?" Marie went into her bedroom, opened the bottom drawer of the dresser, and reaching beneath the pile of receipts and cards and letters, pulled out something that had lain hidden for nearly fifteen years—a tiny sweater, half finished, a ball of pink yarn, and two shiny metal knitting needles.

Angie, already groggy from two sleeping pills, lay on a heavy bath towel on the kitchen table, silent tears running into her hair. The smell of alcohol was strong as Marie doused her hands, then the wicked looking instrument.

Later, she held the sobbing child in her arms until relief, exhaustion and the sleeping pills finally claimed her. Then she carried her to the bed, tucked the covers under the soft little girl chin and called Ruth.

"Angie's here," she said. "She's not feelin' too good. Says she's had cramps all day. Could be this whole thing's a false alarm. . . . No, no need to come over. I put her to bed and she's asleep. Come mornin', she'll be fine."

Then, with the late afternoon sun slanting across the yard, she rolled the tiny sweater that would never be finished, the pink yarn and the hateful metal probes into the bloody towel, took a shovel from the shed, and buried the whole bundle deep in the garden where nothing ever grew.

A Vision Of Violets

"It happens, you know," I said into the silence that stretched like a canopy over the breakfast table.

Curt sat, a forkful of scrambled eggs halfway to his mouth. Then he carefully placed the fork back on the plate and laid his napkin on the table. The scrape of the chair was harsh in the quiet kitchen. At the door, he turned and looked at me, his mouth a thin line.

I watched him go, heard the screen close behind him with a soft little *whoosh*. Outside the sun shone, birds chirped, and the handkerchief-sized yard was a mosaic of grass and violets. I tried to remember their fragrance, but in the shabby kitchen, all I could smell was the eggs getting cold on Curt's plate. I looked at the dry toast in my hand, took a bite and forced it past the nausea.

I had done the test twice, although I didn't need that little pink stick—or three years of nursing school—to tell me I was pregnant. My breasts were swollen and tender, my stomach just beginning to firm and round.

Curt's reaction was about what I expected. I worked part-time at the clinic down on Front Street, and the simple truth was that we depended on my salary to make ends meet. After taxes and bus fare, it just about covered his child support.

"You'll have nothing but grief," my mother had warned, the Old World accent thickening as her voice rose. "A divorced man. And him with two kids yet." She shook her head, her hands twisting in her lap. "Another woman's leavings, another woman's kids. And him old enough to be your papa."

"Mom! He's thirty-six. I'm twenty-two. He'd have been pretty precocious, don't you think?"

"Precocious? What's that, one of your fancy schmancy college words?" Then her hands stilled and her face softened. "You're young, Rachel. Pretty. You can afford to be choosy. Think, child, think."

Was it, I wondered, her own marriage she regretted? My dad, ten years her senior, ruled the household with an iron hand, believing that was his Christian duty. And yet, she took on so when he died—took on, I remembered, like a child left to fend for herself.

"I *have* thought, Mom. I've done nothing *but* think these last few days. I love him, and I'm going to marry him."

She half rose from the chair and shook her finger in my face. "You mark my words, missy. Nothing but grief."

The funny thing was, Mom had always liked Curt. He and Wilda, his first wife, lived across the street from us when I was a kid. After Dad got sick, Mom depended on "that nice young man" to take care of the leaky faucets and the stubborn old furnace. She loved Curt, the handyman; it was Curt, the future son-in-law, she couldn't stand.

It *was* hard. I dreaded to hear the phone ring. Curt's kids always needed something. Something expensive that Wilda couldn't—or wouldn't—pay for out of the child support.

Like yesterday. Kyle called. Collect, of course. He needed new sneakers. "Pumps, Dad. Please. All the other kids . . ."

Sure. Eighty dollar tennis shoes, and I had been scrounging my clothes from garage sales.

They were nice kids, Kyle and Kaylee, all-American kids with perfect teeth and perfect manners, who had learned how to push all the right buttons. Curt would get that look, and I knew what he was thinking. Early on he told me about a childhood so deprived it was beyond my ability to imagine it. Abandoned with five children under six, his mother coped the best she could.

"My kids will never have to do without," he said, and my heart broke for all he had missed, all I could never give him. My parents, both of them, were stern, but I never doubted they loved me, never went hungry for either food or affection. I dreamed of having our own baby, imagining that, in sharing that childhood, Curt would recover part of his own. Surely, someday we could have a family of our own. But not now. Oh, Lord, not now.

I scraped the eggs into the disposal, holding my breath against the smell. The window was open, and April drifted in, fresh and sweet. The grass, ankle-high, was long overdue for its first cutting, but I always felt a vague sadness as, swath by swath, the violets disappeared.

I hadn't even gotten around to picking the ritual bouquet for the sunny kitchen windowsill. *Bringing in the spring*, Mom always called it. As a child, I picked handfuls of the purple blooms, mangling the delicate stems in my sweaty fist, until every jelly glass in the house was filled; until Mom gently suggested I leave some for the neighbors to enjoy.

Outside, the sun still shone; the birds still chirped. Curt sat, legs spread, on the concrete apron between the garage and the back porch with pieces of the old and ailing lawnmower around him. He looked up, tried to smile, and shuffled over to the door. Hurt and angry, I stood, my hand flat against the screen. He fitted his fingers to mine, the mesh between us.

"I'm sorry, honey." A sound, half growl, half groan, came from between his teeth. "I want kids. You know I do. But we're just scraping by now. How can we afford a baby?"

I turned away, determined not to cry. I knew all that. But I certainly didn't get pregnant all by myself, and now that I was, what did he expect me to do about it? I didn't dare ask, couldn't even think about the obvious answer.

It had happened, I knew, in a cabin in the mountains, with a winter moon hanging in the sky and the snow, seductive as a kiss, drifting down through the trees. Our first anniversary. If I were forced to choose between Curt and this tiny growing thing, would there be a second?

The screen opened, closed, and he was behind me, his hands on my shoulders. "Rachel? Rachel, honey, look at me."

Reluctantly I turned.

"I love you, sweetheart. Love you so much." He drew me to him, and I yielded, just a little. "I wanted to give you everything—the sun and the moon and the stars—and look at what you got." His eyes swept the crowded duplex. "My God, where would we put a baby? In a dresser drawer? That's what my mother did, one right after another."

Another time I might have held him close, shared his pain, but right now I had bruises of my own to tend. "So what are we going to do?" I said.

"Wait a year, honey. Another year and you'll have your degree, and by then, things will have settled down with the kids."

Yeah, right, I thought, pulling away. *Another year and Kyle will be in high school, and that's when it really starts.*

"Wait a year?" I said. "Great idea. Only trouble is, you're about eight weeks too late."

He stood looking at me for the longest time, then turned and again walked out into the sunshine.

I wished I could make sense of it, make it all fit, but it didn't. It never seemed to balance out—the young girls at the clinic, single and pregnant and desperate—other women, wives, *not* pregnant and desperate. And now, here I was, pregnant after just one unguarded moment. My friend Carmen had tried for months, turned her bedroom into a laboratory where sex was dictated not by passion, but by the calendar and the thermometer. And my own mother. How often had I heard her at night, praying, *Just one more baby. Please, God, just one more.*

I remembered her coming home from the hospital that last time, red-eyed, empty-armed, remembered my dad saying, "Hush, Nadia, it is God's will." Then, in a rare gesture of tenderness, he drew us both into his arms. "We have one healthy daughter. It is enough, yes? It is enough." As he turned to go up the stairs, I realized, young as I was, that he had suddenly grown old.

I spread the morning paper out on the table and turned to the classifieds. Sunlight splashed the columns, setting the ugly words a-shimmer. I shuddered and stuffed the paper in the trash. Then, a memory—one I thought I had buried for good—wormed its way to the surface. That other time, the summer I graduated from high school. My period three weeks late. The long, scalding baths, the frenzied aerobics. And then, finally, the precious, painful flood. For a long time, I dreamed of faceless babies floating in row after row of steaming tubs.

I shook my head as if to rid it of a bothersome insect. *Get a grip, Rachel.* My mind, my training, told me those old wives' remedies were unlikely to affect a healthy pregnancy.

And yet, I wondered. I would always wonder.

Without thinking, I picked up the phone and dialed Mom. I was tired, so tired, and hearing her voice, I wished I could crawl through the line and into her lap.

"What's wrong?" she said, right off the bat.

"Nothing's wrong, Mom. I just wanted to say hello."

I wanted to tell her, tell her all of it, tell her that maybe she was right, that maybe I had gotten into more than I knew how to handle, but I couldn't.

"You sound funny. You sure you're not sick?"

I wanted to hear her say, as she did when I was little, *There, there, baby, it'll be all right. You'll see.*

"I'm fine, Mom," I said.

"What about Curt? You two having trouble?"

"Mom! Curt's fine, I'm fine. Everybody's fine. Okay?"

I listened as she told me how the paper boy always threw the paper in the yard, the garbage man was always either too late or too early, and Mrs. Baird next door was having trouble with her foot.

"I can't remember if she said it was her right or her left, but anyway . . ."

"Mom, I have to go. I really do."

Later, bereft, I wedged myself into my old childhood rocker and cried until I thought I might never stop.

The morning was gone, the sun just beginning to creep toward the west, when finally I went to the window, stood staring out at the scrap of lawn through swollen eyes. Curt, shirtless, yanked the cord of the old mower again and again. The grass, tall and uncouth, was purple with violets.

I molded the curve of my stomach with my hands, felt a tremor of wonderful, terrible anticipation as I imagined it blowing up, bigger and bigger, like a balloon, like the women I saw every day at the clinic. Pregnant and awkward and miserable. Yet, later they came with flaccid bellies and proud shy smiles, laid their marvelous, mewling creations like offerings on the examining table. And those slick-skinned wonders lay there, arms and legs waving like fronds of some exotic plant.

Yearning, swift and strong, filled me.

Curt pulled the cord once more. I heard the savage roar, saw the first flower heads fall beneath the blades. Then I was at the door, wrenching the knob, crying, stumbling down the steps until I stood in his path. "Wait!" I said, burying my face in my hands. "Just wait."

He turned the mower off, tipped my chin up with one finger, but I jerked away.

"I'm going to have this baby," I said. "With or without you, I'm having this baby."

He looked at the car in the driveway, the gasoline can on the sidewalk, everywhere but at me. "Then I guess we'll have the baby," he said softly. "I can't imagine life without you."

My hands gripped his forearms, shaking him gently. "Curt, look at me. This is *our* baby—yours and mine. We'll be okay. I don't need the sun and the moon and the stars. And the kids don't need everything they ask for either. Heck, they probably don't even *want* everything they ask for."

I smiled and jostled him again, delicately, just enough to settle the jagged pieces of his past into their proper place. "Hey, how much can one tiny baby cost? Besides, once the little tyke is walking, we can always put him to work."

His mouth twisted into a half-hearted grin. "At least, he won't be bugging me for eighty dollar tennis shoes."

"Not for a while anyway," I said.

We began to laugh, the uncontrolled, exhilarated laughter of narrow escapes. Then I was in his arms, the curve of my belly, tentative as a new moon, sheltered and warm between us.

Sunday Drivers

Wes slouches behind the wheel of our—soon to be his—2006 Toyota. I'm plastered against the opposite door, staring at the sullen West Virginia winter: dirty gray snow, dirty gray sky, an altogether nasty Sunday afternoon. Driving east on Indian Ridge Road, gravel spurting from the tires, we declare our marriage dead, agree on final arrangements. He gets the car and the payment book; I get the waterbed, the TV, and the antique chest we found at a yard sale that first spring. It's all settled. There's nothing more to say, so we ride in silence.

The uneven rhythm of radials on wet and rutted blacktop jars like broken promises. *Do you, Wesley . . . for better, for worse, for richer, for poorer . . .* I do. *Do you, Sharon . . . in sickness or in health, to love and to cherish.* I do.

I do—but only until some dreary Sunday, driving east on Indian Ridge Road.

The road rises so sharply that we seem to be driving right into the sky. Suddenly, muddy tires, a truck, huge and red and rusted, looms above us. Too late, Wes jerks the wheel to the right. Metal scrapes metal. Cables snap, wood splinters as we crash through the guardrail. Then we're airborne.

I see rocks, a frozen creek bed. *I'll be damned*, I think. *'Til death do us part, in spite of ourselves.* The car bounces hard. Once. Twice. A tire explodes. We tilt on two wheels, bounce again, finally stop, wedged against a tree.

We stare at each other. Wes unfastens his seat belt with fingers that have not yet begun to tremble. He rains indiscriminate kisses on my hair, my face, mumbles love gibberish into my ear.

It's too soon to understand what is happening. I just listen, and hang on for dear life.

Silent Night, Lonely Night

Judd McClanahan stood at the curtainless window of his apartment, watching the kaleidoscope of falling snow against colored lights. Outside it was Christmas Eve, but in this drab room there was no sign of it. No tree, no candles, no brightly wrapped presents. No toys to be assembled. Worst of all, no Jenny and Josh. No Beth.

This time last year he had been tucking the kids, fresh-scrubbed and rosy from their baths, into bed, reading them the story about the mean old Grinch. But somehow, in a few short months, he had gotten hopelessly lost, taken a wrong turn, and left Christmas, along with everything else that mattered, behind in that neat house on Palmer Avenue. And for what? "For nothing," he muttered, giving the faded sofa bed a kick.

Nothing . . . nothing . . . nothing. The word seemed to echo in the room. He shivered and turned the thermostat up a notch, although he knew it wouldn't help. The chill he felt came from inside.

It seemed to him that there had been no summer that year. In April, when the tender petals of the magnolia tree began to unfold, freezing rain encased them in a crystal shell until they melted away with the ice. In May, just short of his thirty-eighth birthday, came that wintry blast to his spirit when nothing seemed right—not his job, not his marriage. Nothing. And Samantha blew into his life, as brittle and beautiful as the magnolias. By the time an early frost turned the proud chrysanthemums brown, the madness was over, but it was too late. Beth had filed for divorce, and he was doing solitary penance in this crummy apartment.

Tonight especially, he wished, oh, how he wished, he could go back and do it right. He took a beer from the refrigerator and picked a frozen dinner at random from the freezer. Salisbury steak. Damn, why had he bought that? He hated Salisbury steak. He slid the tray into the oven and took a long swallow of beer.

He thought of other Christmases, the house aglow with lights, fragrant with pine and spices, the tree decorated, the table festive and full of good things. Carols on the stereo. By now, Jenny and Josh would be wound so tight they'd be bouncing off the walls. And unflappable Beth. He could just hear that soft little voice, "Better settle down, kids, or there'll be nothing but lumps of coal in those stockings." Funny thing was, they *would* settle down. There was something about that voice. That voice. God, he had to hear it. He had to talk to her.

He picked up the phone and dialed the first five numbers, then hung up. He couldn't call her. What was there to say? *Sorry, babe, it didn't mean a thing?* It didn't, but what difference did that make? Somehow, it made it even worse. Maybe if he had loved Samantha even a little, he could have forgiven himself.

He had no right to intrude on Beth's holiday. She probably wouldn't talk to him anyway. And why should she? He had betrayed her, broken every promise. Broke her heart. Despicable, that's what he was. He gulped the last of the beer, glared at the empty can as if it contained every sin he ever committed, then crushed it in his fist.

The timer on the oven pinged, and using his sweatshirt as a potholder, he took the aluminum tray from the oven. He peeled the foil back, looked with distaste at the unappetizing lump of meat, the flattened mashed potatoes embossed with the pattern of ice crystals. "Merry Christmas, you jerk," he said aloud. Without sitting down, he forced himself to eat a few forkfuls.

Outside, the snow still fell in soft swirls against the red and green and blue and yellow lights of the street decorations. Carols from the next apartment seeped through the walls. *Silent night, holy night. All is calm* ... But the words turning in his mind were not of hope and joy, but despair. *Silent night, lonely night. All is gone* ... He prowled the cramped room, from the window to the couch, from the couch to the TV. Turn it on. Turn it off. He stood in front of the telephone, willing it to ring, but, of course, it didn't.

Well, he could call his kids, couldn't he? He would see them tomorrow, give them the department store-wrapped gifts he had stashed in the car. But to his way of thinking, Christmas Day was a little sad, even in the good years. Anticlimactic, that's what it was. Christmas Eve—now there was magic for you, the time when all things were possible and dreams could still come true.

When he was a boy, Santa came on Christmas Eve, announced by heavy footsteps on the front porch and bells fading into the crisp night. He never did figure out how his parents had pulled that off without being seen by four sets of eager eyes.

His parents. They were still together after more than forty years. Still held hands, still kissed under the mistletoe when they thought no one was watching. It had been that way for Beth and him, too. Once.

But there was no reason he couldn't call the kids. Sure. He would call and just say hello to Jenny and Josh. No harm in that.

Beth answered, her *Hello* like a soft cooing in his ear. The coldness in him turned to slush as he remembered the scent of her, clean and fresh like the air after a spring rain, the feel of her compact little body in his arms. "Uh . . . hi, Beth. Um . . . Merry Christmas. Just thought I'd call and say *hi* to the kids. Are they in bed?"

Of course, they're in bed, you idiot, he thought, looking at his watch. It was nearly ten o'clock.

"Yep," she said, "Kiddies nestled all snug in their beds. Visions of sugar plums and all that." The soft voice had taken on hard edges, and he winced.

The thought of those warm little bodies in new Christmas pajamas filled him with a sweet ache. "Well, uh, sorry. I didn't realize it was so late. I just wanted to, you know, tell them goodnight." In the background he heard music, laughter. A man's voice. Oh, God, she was having a party. He shouldn't have called. How could he have thought a woman like Beth would be spending Christmas Eve alone? He wondered if she was wearing that sexy red thing she wore last year.

"Sounds like you're busy," he said, an edge creeping into his own voice. "Sorry to have bothered you." He imagined her looking up at someone tall and male, her laugh fizzing and breaking into tiny bubbles like champagne.

"No problem." There was a long silence; then, "Merry Christmas, Judd."

"Yeah, you, too, Beth. Merry Christmas."

Merry Christmas, Judd. Merry Christmas, Judd. He repeated it softly as he hung up the receiver, trying to capture her exact inflection. Was it his imagination, wishful thinking, or did he hear something more than a polite brush-off? Did she maybe draw the *Judd* out just a little, like she used to when she was feeling playful?

Fool. Fool, fool, fool. He was the biggest fool, the king of them all.

He resumed his aimless prowling and thought of the wolf at the zoo, how it paced the fence line, up and back, up and back; how Josh, seeing the misery of that caged wild thing, had cried. That was the same day it all came crashing down.

"Who's Samantha?" Beth had asked.

Just like that. *Who's Samantha?* And the earth stopped turning, and his heart forgot to beat. He tried to plead temporary insanity, which was as close to the truth as he could get, but Beth would have none of it. Their marriage was over.

Now, on this barren Christmas Eve, he opened the refrigerator, searching for something to still the gnawing in his belly. Bread, but nothing to put on it. Probably moldy anyway. No milk. Orange juice carton, empty. He tossed it in the trash and poked at the congealed mess still sitting on the table. Hot, the TV dinner had been unappealing; cold, it was downright revolting.

He took his jacket from the doorknob and shrugged into it. It wasn't that late; surely he could find someplace open. Maybe a McDonald's or at least a convenience store. They always seemed to be open. One thing he knew for sure; if he stayed in this apartment, he'd go crazy.

The stores were dark, the streets deserted. The snow had stopped, and stars spattered the sky. He drove slowly, aimlessly, the headlights glittering on an unbroken expanse of white. When he found himself turning onto Palmer Avenue, he had to admit that it would take a whole lot more than a Big Mac to fill the emptiness in him.

He didn't want to see the lights, hear the music and the voices and the laughter spilling out of the house, but he couldn't help himself. He wondered whose cars he would see in the driveway. The Burke's station wagon, for sure. Probably the Nolan's Toyota, and, of course, that snazzy little Mazda that belonged to Beth's sister, Jan. That guy in

Beth's office. The one with the Corvette. Judd had seen the way he looked at her. Would he be there? His hands tightened on the steering wheel.

It was a nice neighborhood. Friendly. Looked like there were several parties in progress, but when he came to the familiar split level, there were no cars in the driveway, no footprints in the new snow on the sidewalk. Except for the glow of Christmas tree lights and the faint flicker of the TV, the house was dark.

He parked across the street and sat there, waiting—waiting for what he didn't know. *Like some lovesick kid*, he thought, rubbing his eyes with the heels of his hands. *What was that song? Oh, yeah.* "On the Street Where She Lives." How many times had he watched that movie with Beth tucked into the curve of his arm, the kids tumbling over them like puppies?

He always thought that guy in the movie was a loser, a clown, standing there on the sidewalk singing his fool head off. And now he, Judd McClanahan, sat in a parked car on Christmas Eve, hoping to catch a glimpse of the woman he loved, getting as close to her as he dared. He shook his head at such adolescent foolishness.

His chest tightened as a shadow moved across the window. Even through the curtain, he could tell she wasn't wearing the slinky red number, but the fuzzy pink robe he had given her, how many years ago? When she tried it on that first Christmas, he had jokingly told her she looked like a sunburned polar bear, and she rewarded him with that bubbly laugh and an elbow to the ribs.

A spasm of love and loss, so sharp he doubled over the steering wheel, shook him. He knew at that moment he would get down on his knees and beg, crawl if he had to, but somehow he would win her back. After all, wasn't that what Christmas was all about? About love and hope? And the promise of redemption?

He slid out of the car, closed the door and stood for a minute taking in the stillness of the night. Then he walked across the street, up the sidewalk, through the pristine snow, never looking back.

Rose In Winter

Rose stands at the window watching the first snow of the season fall in silent patterns. It covers the tufts of grass in the straggly lawn, carpets the cracked sidewalk. Tears pool in the hollows under her eyes and trickle down her wrinkled face like rivulets seeking new channels. Cassie is coming tomorrow, and that alone is reason to cry.

She leans her head against the glass. Soothed by the icy cold, she scoops the cat from her chair and settles into the cushions, which over the years have become a perfect negative of head and back and rump.

So . . . big sister Cassie is coming. *Humph*, she thinks. *More like Queen Cassandra*. Rose knows just how it will be. Cassie will sail into the room on a wave of perfume, her hair, dyed witch black, sprayed hard as a helmet, her feet crammed into pointy-toed shoes. "Rosie, dear, how are you?" she will say, her cool kiss leaving a trail of red, red lipstick across Rose's cheek. Not waiting for an answer, she will clatter about, stuffing things into that blasted bag she always carries. Then, when she has packed Rose's gowns and slippers and good dresses—but none of the things that really matter—she will say, "Come, Rosie dear. We really must go."

"Clairemont is a lovely care facility," Cassie had said on the phone a few days ago. "You're lucky to get in. Without my influence . . ."

Now Rose's face puckers into a knot of misery. "Care facility?" she says to the cat. "It's a nursing home!"

She looks around her. The room is dark and musty, cluttered with the accumulation of almost fifty years. Once her nose would have wrinkled at the smell of dust and neglect, and her fingers would have itched to get at the sooty walls, but now she sees none of that. What she sees is her chair, her hearth, her window, where all those years ago, she watched her husband trudge off to work, her son come home from school.

But tomorrow Cassie is coming, and who knows if she'll ever see this room, this house again. "What right does she have?" Rose mutters. "What right? Thinks I'm senile, she does. Well, she's older than I am. Older by a good five years. And if she thinks I'm dotty, she should take a good look at herself. I don't know what else you could call a woman her age who parades around in those get-ups she wears."

Rose's imagination breaks free and runs away with her, bolts across the boundary of the foreign world she will enter tomorrow. She sees a strange empty room, strange empty faces, hears feeble voices crying out, smells urine and death and decay. In despair and frustration she closes her eyes and whispers, "There's nothing wrong with me! Why can't they understand that? I just have a little trouble talking. If they wouldn't rush me, give me time to collect myself..."

Absently, she strokes the ancient cat that occupies her lap. "Poor Mister Cat," she murmurs. "What's to become of you?" When she talks to herself, as she often does, or when she talks to the cat, the garbled speech that has plagued her since her stroke last summer untangles. And if there are long pauses as she searches for a word, if she sometimes calls a frying pan a flowerpot, or a comb a rake, the cat doesn't mind, and she doesn't notice.

She has lived that summer morning over a hundred times in her mind. What did she do wrong? She was working in the garden, early, before the sun became too hot, when suddenly the lettuce and beans and tomatoes began to waver, and her entire right side seemed to disappear. The hoe dropped from her hands, and she sank to the ground like a scarecrow loosed from its pole.

Her next memory was of coarse white sheets and tubes in her arms and nose. And Cassie bending over her, *Oh, Rosie dearing*, and crying crocodile tears. Her son Luke was there, too, all the way from Oregon.

"What are you doing here?" she asked. He leaned closer, trying to understand. Then, eyebrows raised, he looked at the nurse, who shrugged and shook her head.

In a few days Luke had to go back home. Cassie, having done her sisterly duty, disappeared, and Rose was alone with the multitude of doctors and nurses and therapists and aides. They were kind, most of them, but they all, even the best, behaved as if she had lost her mind and her hearing, as well as her speech.

One day as she sat in her wheelchair in the hall waiting to be taken back to her room, a doctor lounged against the wall beside her, talking into a pocket recorder. "Patient is a white female, 71 years..." he stopped to count, and then continued, "seven months. Experienced CVA on 23 June this year."

It was a stroke, she tried to say. *Call it what it was*. But the words that were in her head would not come out of her mouth.

She might have been a sack of laundry sitting there as he went on. "Patient has mild weakness on right side, moderate to severe aphasia."

You mean I can't talk right, you white-coated jackass, she wanted to shout. *Look at me! I'm not 'patient.' I'm Rose!* But the words hung there in her mind, burning in her brain. *I'm Rose.*

Remembering the frustration, the humiliation, she begins to cry again. Finally, she dries her eyes, blows her nose and picks up the photograph beside her chair. The silver frame is tarnished, the glass dusty and flyspecked, but she sees only the handsome young soldier and his bride on their wedding day. She's a plain little thing, with plain brown hair and a mischievous grin. Her dress is white lawn, cobwebbed with lace. Rose can almost feel the high collar scratching her neck. She looks at the hand holding the picture, thick-knuckled and spotted with age. How can she be so old, when such a short time ago she was young?

She touches the face of her husband. "Cassie's coming tomorrow, Matt. She says I have to leave. She says I have to go to one of those places. Oh, sweetheart, what am I going to do?"

Do you always do everything The Queen tells you to? That's what Matt always called Cassie—The Queen. She hears his voice, gentle and chiding, as plain as if he were standing beside her.

Does she always do as Cassie says? Well, yes, she usually does, more from habit than anything else, she supposes. There was that one time, though. Her face crinkles in a wicked grin.

She would have been seven or eight that year. Papa had given her a quarter to buy a birthday present for Mama. Cassie, being older, had fifty cents.

"Now, Rose, you mind Cassie," Mama said as they went out the door. It was always *Rose, you mind Cassie*. Never, *Cassie, be nice to your sister*. Never, *Cassie, don't bully your sister*.

Rose had been a change-of-life baby, a mistake. She could never remember a time when she hadn't known that. Cassie was the child Mama wanted, prayed for, thought she would never have. Cassie was Mama's world, petted and pampered and adored. Then, plain little Rose came along, a fretful, colicky baby, a problem right from the start.

Once out of sight, Cassie grabbed her hand and jerked her along. When they reached The Emporium, just a few blocks away, it took Cassie no time at all to pick out some trinket for Mama—Rose can't remember what—and an assortment of bright hair ribbons for herself. Rose searched every aisle. She knew the perfect present was there somewhere, if only she could find it.

"Hurry up, Rosie; we don't have all day," Cassie said. Before long, she was nudging Rose along, stepping on her heels every few minutes. "Come on, dummy. Just pick something. It doesn't matter."

But it did matter. It mattered a lot. Rose had a quarter, a small fortune, and she wasn't going to be rushed, even though Cassie propelled her along with a hand in the middle of her back.

Then Rose stopped suddenly. Her lips formed a silent *Ohhh*. There on the counter was Mama's present. In a miniature basket, under a pouf of cellophane and ribbon, peach soaps nestled in green tissue. Rose picked it up, paid for it, and cradled it in both hands all the way home. Maybe this time Mama would be pleased. Maybe Mama would hug her and tell her it was the best present she had ever gotten. Maybe this time she would say, "Rose, I love you." Maybe she would.

Later that afternoon, Rose was sitting cross-legged on her bed, sniffing the sweet peachy smell through the cellophane, when Cassie came in. Her shiny black curls were tied with one of the new ribbons, and she held the present she had bought in front of her.

"Here," she said. "You can have this. I want that." And she pointed to Rose's treasure.

Give Cassie Mama's wonderful present she had picked out all by herself? Oh, she couldn't. She really couldn't. "No," she said, holding the basket behind her back. "No!"

No? Cassie was not familiar with the word. She lunged at her sister, one hand grabbing for the basket, the other for Rose's hair.

Remembering, Rose quivers with laughter. "Land sakes, Cat, I bit her! Yes, I did. Got a licking for it too. But by cracky, I kept what was mine."

"I kept what was mine," she repeats softly. She looks around her at the chronicle of her years—the pictures lining the walls, crowding every flat surface; Matt's books on the shelves, his glasses on the table by his chair just where he left them. Baby shoes, cracked and yellowed, all she has left of frail little Mark. Even the paths worn in the carpet, where she walked away long nights with fussy babies, where she paced, waiting for her husband to come home after an argument when she wasn't sure he would.

She sits in silence, lost in the past. Then, "Scat, Cat," she says, shooing the cat from her lap. "I've got work to do. It's high time we teach Sister Cassie a new word." She chuckles and shakes her finger at the cat. "And this time, there'll be no biting. Understand? No biting."

Settling deep into the chair, she squeezes her eyes shut and carefully arranges words on the blackboard of her mind. She imagines the feel of them in her mouth, pressing against her teeth and tongue, imagines her lips shaping the sounds as she frees them, one by one. Then, she practices, over and over until she is sure they will come out just right tomorrow, when Cassie comes. "No, I'm staying here. No. I'm staying here. No! I'm staying here!"

Finally satisfied, she rises and turns the fire up high so the grate glows red, radiating light and warmth against the evening chill. She pulls her chair to the window, sees the sky change from gray-blue to black. The snow has stopped. A watery moon oozes through the clouds, and one lonely star flickers above the horizon.

"I'm staying here," she says softly. With sweater drawn tight over her bony chest, she watches the light from her window paint a shimmering path across the snow.

Aphasia

My father—Daddy I call him
though I'm past sixty—
tries, tries so hard to tell me
something.
And when I cannot understand
the words come, salty and plain,
and his face crumples,
for these are not words
he would choose,
not words he would use in the presence
of his eldest daughter.

My father—Daddy—has many friends.
They come singly and in pairs,
toss words like pebbles
into the silent sea,
and failing to fill it
they disappear
one
by one
by one.

Alone, adrift, he trolls for names
of people and places and things.
Slick and silver as minnows
they hide in deep pools,
dart out to tease him.

And I too am afflicted,
for the words I want to say,
the words he needs to hear,
elude me.

I chase their shadow,
cup my hands to catch them—
but when I do, they are changelings,
sorry, misshapen creatures
that disappear in a swirl of silt.

"Swallow your pills," I say.
"Swallow them."

Blood Kin

Gray afternoon light filtered through coal-grimed windows as two women, sisters-in-law, bent over a beat-up card table working a jigsaw puzzle. "You wouldn't think snow would make a noise, would you?" Marie's fleshy arms jiggled as she gathered possibilities in her hand, then tried to fit them, one by one, into an oddly shaped space.

Ruth sucked on a cigarette and listened for a moment before replying. "Kinda whispers, don't it?"

"So when's Angie coming in?"

Ruth tried a piece of sky and laid it back down. "Beats me. Says she's bringing me a surprise."

Marie chuckled. "Seems like she was always bringing you surprises."

"Don't remind me." Ruth coughed and grimaced. "Can't think of any of them that was good."

Piece by piece, a riot of pink and red roses grew against an impossibly blue sky as the women worked in silence. Early winter darkness had already crept into the corners of the room when a pickup truck chugged up the rutted lane and clattered to a stop. The driver, a grizzled old man, battered as the truck he drove, swung a duffel bag to the sidewalk, and a young woman wearing baggy jeans and a denim jacket got out. The wind, bitter now, whipped strings of dingy blond hair across her face as she watched the truck disappear in a cloud of exhaust. The sleeves of an over-sized jacket covered her hands, and in her arms she clasped a large blanket-wrapped bundle.

"Dear God," Ruth exclaimed as she peered through the limp curtains. "She's either dragging in another one of her orphan animals, or that's a baby she's a-carrying." For the first time in her life, she hoped it was an animal. Stern-faced, she watched her only child slog through ice-crusted puddles to the porch.

Marie hobbled to the door, her legs protesting the weight of years of fried potatoes and beans cooked with fat meat. Angie, holding the bundle close, stood in the doorway looking as if she might turn and run.

"Well, for heaven's sake, Angela, come on in," Marie said.

Ruth said nothing.

The baby, who looked to be five or six months old, struggled to free herself of the blanket and her mother's arms.

"Mama, Aunt Marie, this is Jade." Angie put the child down on the floor and knelt beside her. "Say *hi* to Grandma, sweetheart. Can you say hi?"

A tiny hand waved a backwards bye-bye.

Ruth stood in silence for a minute, taking in the tight dark curls, the dusky skin. "Grandma, my ass," she said turning her back.

"Well, Angie, it's been a long time. How you been?" Marie's voice was too loud.

The young woman shifted from one foot to the other. "Okay, I guess. Been out West, you know."

Ruth, her back still to the door, muttered, "Looks to me like you been in bed. Been in bed with a—"

"Don't say it, Ma," Angie warned. Then, pleading, "Please, Ma."

Laughing nervously, Marie stooped to pick up the child. "Why, she's a pretty little thing. Pretty as a picture. Look, Ruth. I believe she's got your eyes." The eyes, huge and liquid, the color of sorghum, were nothing at all like Ruth's gray ones.

Ruth whirled around. "I'll just say this one thing, Angela. You snuck off in the middle of the night—left school, threw away a scholarship just like it was nothing. I ain't heard from you but what? Once or twice since? Now you come in here dragging a half-breed kid, and you expect me to be happy about it? Well, I ain't. I was better off laying awake at night, wondering if you was alive or dead."

The whisper of snow turned to a murmur as the wind picked up. Angie gathered the whimpering child in her arms, picked up the blanket and the bag, and laid a hand on the doorknob. Then she bowed her head, shrugged and turned to face her mother.

"Ma . . . Mama. I've no place to go. We'll not give you any trouble. I promise." She tucked a strand of hair, lifeless as broom straw, behind her ear. "Please, Ma."

"We figured you'd stay a spell," Marie said. "I got the bed all made up."

The two women had shared the same house since Ruth's husband disappeared with a waitress from town. They rarely disagreed, but now Ruth shot a venomous look at her sister-in-law. "Well, then," she said, "sounds like it's all settled."

"Ruth!" Marie said through clenched teeth as the door to the tiny bedroom closed. "How could you? Your girl comes home after all this time, and you act like that! And that sweet *baby*. You didn't no more than glance at her. For God's sake, what's past is past. Let it be."

"Yes, she's home, all right. Packing a load of trouble, too. I'd bet on it. You know what it was like, Marie. All at once, seemed like she went to hell in a hand basket. One day, butter wouldn't melt in her mouth, and next thing you know . . . God only knows who that baby belongs to."

"*That baby* belongs to Angie," Marie retorted, sweeping the half finished puzzle into the box. "She's kin, like it or not."

Supper was a tense affair, and breakfast, no better. Later, while Marie fed the chickens and Jade napped, Angie sidled into the kitchen where Ruth stood, dishrag in hand, staring out the window.

"Ma, there's something I gotta tell you."

"Figures," Ruth said, grim-faced.

"I already told you we got no place to go. Jade's daddy—" She broke off and looked around as if wondering how she had wound up back where she started. Her face, aged by years of living fast and hard, softened as she went on. "I loved him, Mama. And he loved me. Maybe the only person ever did, except maybe Aunt Marie."

Ruth winced. She loved her daughter. Of course she did. But there was a wall between them. Had been for as long as she could remember. She envied Marie, sometimes blamed her for spoiling Angie.

Angie tugged on a strand of hair as she continued. "He had AIDS. We both knew he was going to die, but I guess I never really believed it. Anyway, I have . . . I have what he had. I'm probably going to die, too. Jade's fine, thank God." Her voice cracked, and she stopped as if surprised by the prayer that had escaped from some long forgotten corner of her soul. Then, still shaken, "Mama . . . I'm not asking for myself; it's for Jade. If I get sick, I have to know she's with someone who'll take care of her."

There was an ache somewhere in Ruth's middle and a moan rose in her throat, but she ground it out, just as she ground out her cigarette in the overflowing ashtray. "So. Your chickens come home to roost, did they?" She lit another cigarette. "You think I don't know? You think I ain't heard how you get that particular disease?" Her words were like acid, boiling up from some great vat of bitterness, burning everything they touched.

Angie stood silent and stricken, pale, her eyes huge and full of tears. She swallowed hard. "God, Ma, I didn't know you hated me that much. Okay. I've done wrong, made more mistakes than most folks do in a lifetime. Maybe I deserve how you feel; maybe I deserve to die. But what about Jade? She's done nothing. She's innocent."

"Jade," Ruth muttered, scrubbing the worn counter. "What kinda name's that?"

"She's your granddaughter, Ma. Your blood. What about her?"

"Don't look like no kin of mine." Ruth turned her back, then whirled and grabbed her daughter's shoulders, her bony fingers sinking into the wasted flesh. "You had it all, Angie. Pretty. And smart. You could'a got out of this God-forsaken valley, been somebody. And what did you do? You threw it away." Ruth's throat was so full of tears she was choking, but she went on. "You threw it away, just like it was nothing."

The door scraped across worn linoleum as Marie came in, flushed from the cold. She hung her jacket on a peg and stood for a moment, watching the scene before her, wondering what to do about the two people she loved most in all the world, knowing in her heart she had played a part in their agony.

She remembered that other time when Angie, little more than a child, had cried in her arms, begging, "Help me, Aunt Marie. Please help me." And Marie *had* helped her in the only way she knew. But now, staring over Angie's head into the garden, empty except for the secrets buried there, she realized she had only traded one tragedy for another. There were ghosts in that garden. She could see them now—a tiny, bloody bundle that would have been a child, and the Angie that might have been—the Angie who had also died that day.

Marie's rough hands smoothed Angie's lifeless hair. "Forgive me, sweetheart," she whispered. "I meant to give you a second chance, and I only gave you this. I'm so sorry." She stepped back and held the girl at arms length, shaking her gently. "Now, don't you worry none about Jade. I'll look out for that sweet angel."

Tears polished Angie's face as she buried herself in the comfort of Marie's arms. "Oh, Aunt Marie," she choked, "that's what Jade's daddy called me. *My sweet Angel.* Not Angie or Angela. It was always Angel, right from the start." She picked at a hangnail. "I miss him, Aunt Marie. He made me feel . . . good. And decent."

Across the room, Ruth scrubbed another layer from the faded countertop. *Angel.* The wrinkles around her mouth softened as she heard the echo of her own voice, whispered into her baby's ear. *You're Mama's own sweet Angel. Yes, you are.* Where had it gone wrong? She couldn't say just when or why, but by the time Angie could put two words together, they were constantly butting heads.

Day by day Ruth watched her daughter grow paler and weaker. Marie cooked and coaxed and coaxed and cooked. "Try to eat something, honey," she would say. "You've got to keep your strength up." And again, "I made rice pudding. You always liked that. Take a bite, sweetheart, just one bite. It'll make you feel better."

Ruth watched as Marie helped Angie bathe Jade, as she nuzzled the fat little neck, as she brushed the dark curls into a smoky halo. One day, as Marie and Angie struggled to get a diaper on the wriggling infant, Ruth heard Angie say, "I knew I could count on you, Aunt Marie. I never could depend on Daddy, and Mama hates me. I don't know what I'd do without you."

Ruth clenched her teeth and swallowed the pain that rose in her throat. She didn't hate her daughter; of course, she didn't hate her. How could you hate your own flesh and blood? She damned the stubborn pride, the generations of ingrained prejudice that held her prisoner. At night she slipped into the bedroom, willing Angie's raspy breathing to go on, sometimes daring to touch the ropes of sweaty hair coiled on the pillow. And always she stopped at the crib where Jade slept, dark fingers curled into pink palms.

Angie disappeared at the end of February, on a day that was more spring than winter, when the maples stood red against a blue sky and the first robins tugged worms from the sodden earth. She didn't say goodbye, left no note, only an empty sweat-soaked bed, and Jade, howling, wet and hungry.

Ruth twisted her apron into a knot as they searched the room for some clue as to where Angie might be headed, but there was nothing. They called the hospital and the morgue and the bus station and the sheriff and the State Police, but Angie was gone, vanished like a puff of smoke.

Winter dribbled into spring and spring into summer. Ruth grieved with the inconsolable grief of one who has thrown away a last chance to forgive—and be forgiven. She couldn't eat, couldn't sleep. In dreams she saw Angie, sick and alone. Angie, dying. Alone.

"I love her," she said over and over to Marie. "She's my daughter; how could I not love her?"

"Of course you do. Angie knows that," Marie rubbed her sister-in-law's shoulders, feeling the fragile bones beneath. "You know Angie. She's tough. She'll come back when she's good and ready."

But by then, Ruth feared it would be too late for all of them.

Jade changed day by day, it seemed. She took a step, then another. Then she was walking, into everything, exploring every inch of the crowded cottage that was within her reach. She chattered to the barn cat through the screen door in a language that only she and the cat understood. She chased rainbows from the crystal that hung in the window, giggling and babbling as she tried to catch them in her chubby fist. Marie lifted the tot to the window, showed her how to spin the crystal so that the room was painted with ever-changing patterns of color. Then, with the child held tightly in her arms, she waltzed around the room, refusing to acknowledge the aching stiffness in her heavy legs.

Ruth, watching them, inhaled the joy and kept it closed tight inside.

She did what was necessary for the child; she changed her and fed her, kept her clean, even forgot at times the strangeness of curly hair and dark skin. Other times, she studied the child, trying to understand how such rare beauty could come from her daughter and the unknown black man. But it was Marie who sang to Jade, cuddled her, rocked her to sleep.

One day in late June, when Marie had gone out to run errands and pick up a few groceries, Ruth heard a thud from the bedroom where Jade napped. "Oh, God," she breathed, realizing instantly that the baby had climbed out of her crib and fallen.

Jade sat on the floor, howling at the top of her lungs, blood dripping from her chin to the floor. Drops of red flecked Marie's housedress as she picked up the screaming child. The wet little face buried itself in her shoulder, and tiny arms went around her neck.

"There, now," Ruth soothed, searching for the source of the blood. With her index finger, she explored the full lower lip. Sharp new teeth had penetrated the tender skin.

Suddenly, it was as though she was holding her daughter, her Angela, before all the disappointments, the waste, when she still had dreams, when she could still believe that her daughter might escape the life that she—and Marie, and all the other women in this valley—had learned to accept. "Oh, God, oh, God," she moaned. "I'm sorry, baby. I'm so sorry."

Jade hiccupped and burrowed her head into Ruth's breast.

Ruth mopped the baby's tears, then her own. "It's all right, Angel," she crooned. "It's all right. Grandma's here."

Cousin Joyce's Second Wedding

Cousin Joyce was never quite the same after Godfrey Burke (Mister God, I always called him) left her waiting at the church in front of the entire town of Felicity, not to mention friends and family from a good fifty miles around. Although why she would have wanted to marry that stuck up mama's boy in the first place, I never could understand. For the life of me, I couldn't picture Joyce and him together.

Oh, sure, the Burkes were pillars of the community and all that. But supercilious Godfrey? He couldn't even cross the street unless his mama told him the light was green. And as far as she was concerned, when it came to her little Godfrey and Joyce, that light was *red*.

She took it real hard, Joyce did. Went a little crazy. We couldn't do a thing with her. Couldn't get her to eat. Couldn't get her out of that poor, bedraggled wedding gown. For days after, she wore it everywhere—shopping at the Piggly-Wiggly, rolling bandages for the Felicity Ladies' Aid. Bowling on Thursday night? I swear this is true—she showed up in that wedding gown! Well, that turned out to be a *big* mistake. She got tangled up in the skirt, and a seven-ten split wasn't the only split she had to worry about that night.

We were real close, being only nine months apart. Joyce always said if my mama hadn't come to help Aunt Edna when she was born, her being such a cute baby and all, I wouldn't even be here. Be that as it may, we were more like sisters, closer than some I could name, and I hated to see her humiliate herself like she was.

"Joyce," I said, "you've *got* to pull yourself together." (Now this had nothing whatsoever to do with what happened at the bowling alley; it was just my way of saying how she was carrying on wasn't normal.) "People are talking. Just who do you think Pastor Carson meant when he asked God to comfort them whose grief had clouded their mind? It wasn't the Widow Jenkins, I can tell you. One look at her, and you can see she's happier than she's been in years."

Well, Joyce turned those big green eyes on me, all innocent and surprised, and it hurt me. It really did. But somebody had to straighten her out, and who better than me, who loved her?

"And do you suppose they wouldn't talk anyway, Silvie?" she came back at me in that soft little voice that made me want to strangle her.

She finally did stop wearing the gown, but did she burn it, or pack it away in her cedar chest, like any normal person would've? Oh, no! Not Cousin Joyce. Put it on a dressmaker's dummy, she did. Set it right in the parlor, where it was the first thing you saw when you stepped in the door.

She was a pretty girl, Joyce was. Long black hair, straight as a poker, and that white skin that seems like a light's shining through it. Everybody figured she'd be married in no time, and, according to Aunt Edna, she had her chances. But Joyce wasn't interested. She took on that tragic look and, you might say, became a legend in her own time. The older ladies made a fuss over her, and the young girls thought it was *so romantic*, even wrote poems about her that got published in the newspaper, not naming names, of course. And the men! Well, as I said, she was a pretty girl.

Nobody saw much of Godfrey. His mother claimed he had gone north to take *a very important position*, but Ed Neeley, who owns the hardware, swears he ran into him over at Cutler, selling cemetery lots door to door.

A few months after Joyce's wedding, I married Buddy Moore, as everyone expected I would, since we had gone steady since tenth grade. After the babies came, just a year apart, I didn't see much of Joyce, not that I didn't still love her like a sister.

So, I was real surprised when, out of the clear blue sky, the phone rang one morning, and Cousin Joyce said, just like it hadn't been weeks since we'd talked, "Get dressed, Silvie. We're going to Charleston."

"What? Joyce, you know I can't go to Charleston. Buddy will be expecting his supper, and then there's the babies."

"You *have* to go. You've got to help me find a wedding dress. We can drop the kids off at Mama's."

I sat down real quick. "What . . . ? Who . . . ?"

But she cut me off in mid-shock. "I'll pick you up in half an hour."

Good grief! What was Joyce going to do with another wedding dress? Wear it bowling? I didn't know whether to call Aunt Edna or what. But one thing I did know, I couldn't have Joyce, in her delicate mental condition, wandering around a big city all by herself.

While I was puzzling on it, the phone rang, and sure enough, it was Aunt Edna, crying and carrying on like somebody had died. "Oh, Silvie, she's sure enough lost her mind. She's been meeting that . . . that person, that Godfrey on the Q T, and now she's bound and determined to marry him. Says it'll be a wedding this town will never forget."

"Oh, God, Aunt Edna! Are you sure? I mean, did she say so herself?"

"Didn't need to. The invitations came not an hour ago, boxes of them, sitting right here on my hall table." She started to read the invitation to me, but couldn't get past *Request the Pleasure of Your Company.*

"You know what'll happen, Silvie. That mother of his hasn't changed one bit, and neither has he. He'll leave her at the altar, just like before. It'll happen, you just wait and see. And we'll be a laughing stock again, all of us. Oooooh, your Uncle Durwood must be turning in his grave."

"What does Pastor Carson have to say about all this? Have you talked to him?"

I could still hear her sobbing on the other end of the line, but she finally came back enough to answer. "Oh, I talked to him, all right. He's smack dab in the middle of it. It was him got them back together!" And Auntie started another round of howling.

"Now, Aunt Edna, calm down," I said, real patient, although I knew the kids were way too quiet. "Aunt Edna?"

"You've got to talk to her, Silvie. She'll listen to you."

By the time I got my favorite lipstick scrubbed off the wall and off Cindy, who's three and should know better, Joyce was at the door.

It took us an hour or more to get to Charleston, and I *tried* to talk to her. The whole way, I tried. "Joyce," I said, "Joyce, honey, I know it's been awful for you, what with all that's happened, but sweetie, Godfrey Burke isn't for you. You *know* that. Forget him. Just forget him and get on with your life."

But she kept right on driving, humming along with the radio like she didn't even hear me.

I reached across the seat and patted her knee, figuring maybe that would get her attention. "I'll tell you what. Let's stop at Maurice's and have us a fancy lunch and talk about this." With any luck, maybe Joyce would come to her senses and I could still get home in time to fix Buddy's supper. He gets real cranky when he's hungry.

But she just shook her head. "I've got to find a dress today. I'm running out of time. See?" And she fished a Bride's Planner out of her purse—FLORIST, CATERER, the works, all neatly filled out in purple ink.

"And just what does Mrs. Burke have to say about all this?"

Joyce giggled. "She doesn't know it yet. But I'm going to send her an invitation."

"You're *what?* Now you listen to me, Joyce Ellen Johnson," I said in my best mother-means-business voice. "You can't *do* this. Remember what happened last time? He's going to make a fool out of you again."

She smiled and gave me that wide-eyed, dreamy look. "You'll to be my matron-of-honor, of course, and your Cindy will make a darling flower girl."

"Joyce, for Pete's sake!"

"You won't even have to buy a dress. You can wear the one you wore before."

We must have hit every store in Charleston, and by three o'clock, I was tired and hungry, and my feet felt like they were on fire. I'd had more than enough of this and was ready to head back up the interstate, with or without Cousin Joyce.

Then she drags me into this little boutique, and there was *the* dress—an ivory lace sheath over beige satin, with a matching satin cummerbund. It fit like it was made for her, clinging to her tiny little waist and hips, the butterfly sleeves falling in graceful cascades over her white arms. My heart turned over to think of my beautiful cousin in that beautiful dress, about to have her heart broken for the second time.

So, there we were on Saturday, June 17—me poured into that awful green gown, Cindy looking like a little angel in mint green, and Joyce, elegant in the ivory lace—standing in the vestibule of the Felicity Baptist Church, waiting for the Wedding March to begin.

A door at the front of the church opened, and in came Pastor Carson, all decked out in his white robe, and beside him, Godfrey Burke. *Mister God.* Even though I knew Joyce was ruining her life, I had to be thankful he had at least shown up this time.

Mary Frances Sweeney was ready at the piano. She poised her hands over the keyboard and brought them down with a vengeance. It was time. Mary Frances pounded away, and I nudged little Cindy forward. I could see Aunt Edna sobbing in the front pew, and if ever a mother had good reason to cry, I figured she did. Poor Aunt Edna. Imagine your only daughter spending the rest of her life with someone like Godfrey Burke. If he didn't chicken out at the last minute, that is.

As I took my place at the front of the church, I could hear the soft swish of lace on satin as Joyce, all alone, came down the aisle. *Nobody was going to give **her** away*, she said.

She walked right up to Godfrey and gave him the most beautiful smile I have ever seen. Then—oh, my God—then! She hooked one finger in the waistband of his tuxedo trousers and stuffed her bouquet in.

Slowly, black hair swinging against the ivory lace, little round hips swaying under it, she walked back up the aisle. Step, slide. Step, slide.

Well, poor Mary Frances. She didn't know what to do, so she just kept playing, and I guess if you stop to think about it, it works either way, *Here comes the bride*, or, *There goes the bride.*

Someone began applauding, and by the time Joyce had reached the third or fourth row, everyone was on their feet, clapping and laughing. Pastor Carson, poor soul, turned the color of fresh putty. Mrs. Burke fainted. And Mister God himself just stood there in a fog, looking at the orchids and stephanotis sprouting out of his pants.

Not much happens in these parts, and folks have long memories. They still tell about that Friday morning back in '98 when Kenny Rogers, or someone who looked a lot like him, stopped by Mamie's Cafe for coffee and one of her famous sticky buns. The way I figure it, twenty, thirty years from now, they'll still be talking about Cousin Joyce's second wedding.

Veronica Lake Jones

Mid-February gloom hung heavy over the gray cottage. Sleet scratched at the windows. A huge old willow, its roots shoved deep in last week's snow, drooped under the weight of yet another winter. In the bird feeder, a cardinal chose a sunflower seed and cracked it open. The slash of red only intensified the gray of house and sky and snow and the freezing rain, which fell like silver pins spilled from a sewing box.

Inside, the house was quiet. A pair of boots stood by the door. The odor of last night's lasagna lingered with garlicky persistence. In the kitchen, a middle-aged black woman sat at the table, a cup of coffee at her elbow. Her head was bowed, her eyes closed. *Oh, Lord,* she prayed, *it's me, your child Vernie. You know me, Lord— better than I know myself, I reckon. You know I'm long past the age to be raisin' kids, especially these little ones. They need so much, Lord. And three of 'em. Lord, I don't think I'm up to it.*

She waited, but there was no answer.

Raising her head, she looked at her five-year-old granddaughter, April, who sat opposite her. The child's light brown skin, the color of an acorn, was chapped and dry, her body thin and underdeveloped. Her eyes, a startling green, were dull and lifeless. Vernie had watched the child play in a tub of warm water the previous night, and for just a moment, the eyes lit up at the rainbow of bubbles around her. She raised a handful to her face and stared into them, perhaps seeing her reflection. Then the light went out and her hand fell listlessly back into the water. Though clean, the little girl still wore the stain of neglect, as if dirt had permeated the skin and settled somewhere beneath. Now, she held her spoon like a weapon and punched at her cereal as if it were something she needed to kill.

"Eat up, honey," Vernie said. "The little 'uns will be up before long."

The call had come early in the morning, just as Vernie got home from work. She set her purse and a small bag of groceries on the counter. "Yes?" she said, trying to remove her coat while holding the phone to her ear. The voice on the other end of the line was warm and friendly, but hurried. "Is this Ms. Veronica Lake Jones?"

"It is, and who's this?" Had to be one of them damned telemarketers; the use of her given name was a dead giveaway. She wondered again what her mam, God rest her soul, could have been thinking—to name her after the glamorous movie star, as fair and blond as she, Vernie, was plain and dark.

She was about to hang up when a voice came back at her. It wasn't a telemarketer.

"This is Susan Wright with the Department of Human Services. Are you the mother of Mary Ann Jones?"

It had been nearly three years since Vernie had seen or heard from her daughter. *Oh, God, no,* she thought. *She's dead. She's o.d'd on them damned drugs, or that asshole she's with has killed her.* Her breath came in short gasps, as if a hole had been ripped in her lungs. "What's happened? Where is she? Where's April?"

"I'm sorry to have to tell you this," the warm voice continued, "but Mary Ann has been arrested, charged with possession of drugs and prostitution. The children are with me. They're safe."

Ridiculous as it was, Vernie felt relief. Her breathing returned to normal. So, Mary Ann wasn't dead; she was in jail. She had been there before. But children? "There must be some mistake. Mary Ann only has one little girl, April."

"April is the oldest; she's five. May is three and June is two. There was a brief pause before the woman continued. "The reason I'm calling . . . You're their closest relative—actually, the only relative I can locate—and I'd like to place them with you, at least for a few days."

Vernie hadn't quite recovered from hearing her daughter's name after all this time; her mind refused to wrap itself around the problem at hand. Instead, she latched on to the ragged edges of the conversation. *April, May and June? Lord a'mighty! Three little 'uns, like pages on a calendar. Only that flighty daughter of mine . . .*

"Ms. Jones?" There was no answer. "Veronica? Are you there?" Vernie roused herself enough to answer.

"I can bring them around in about an hour, if that's all right."

Vernie must have agreed, although she didn't remember, didn't even realize the conversation was over until the dial tone buzzed in her ear. Dazed, she looked around the small but neat room. The walls were lined with pictures—Mary Ann at two, Mary Ann, about the age April was now, standing pigeon-toed, cute and shy in her new Easter outfit. Mary Ann in shorts and a halter-top swinging from the lowest limb of the willow tree. Mary Ann with her hair in an Afro, her face shining like polished walnut, displaying her high school diploma. Mary Ann holding April the summer before her baby turned two, just before she took the child and disappeared into the sewers of the city with that no good boyfriend. Vernie realized now that Mary Ann was probably already pregnant when she left.

Vernie raised April while Mary Ann was off doing whatever it was she did. Would April remember her? She went to the closet and began pulling out sheets and extra quilts. April and the middle one could sleep on opposite ends of the twin bed that had been Mary Ann's. She still had April's crib, and she'd set that up for the little one.

Vernie yawned. Every bone in her body hurt. It had been a long hard night at CareHaven. Mrs. Monroe had had another episode, and by the time her daughter Maggie arrived and got her settled, Mr. Reese in 2B had pulled out his catheter, and his gown and all his bedding had to be changed.

Lillie, the young part-time aide that she had hired to stay with the kids at night opened the door before Vernie could get her key in the lock. She looked almost as bad as Vernie felt. Lillie usually dropped April off at kindergarten on her way home, but today the little girl, still in pajamas, sat in front of the TV watching cartoons.

"School's been cancelled because of the weather, and Junie's sick. I've been up with her most of the night. She threw up a couple of times, but she seems to be better now."

This one should be named Jewel. Or Angel, Vernie thought, as she hugged Lillie goodbye. What a blessing she was.

Vernie stifled a sigh. She had counted on getting an hour or so of sleep before the little ones awoke, but obviously, that wasn't going to happen. She dropped her coat and bag on a chair and went to check on June. The baby lay on her back, mouth open, arms outstretched. "Ah, June Bug," Vernie whispered as she smoothed the soft brown curls from the tiny, slightly flushed forehead, which was warm, but not alarmingly so. She decided to let her sleep.

Back in the living room, April, rapt, leaned forward, giggling at the antics of SpongeBob SquarePants and Gary, his pet snail. May sat on the other end of the couch, unblinking, unsmiling, clutching the Beanie Baby rabbit she had brought with her that first day. Vernie sat down between them, drawing the two girls to her. April settled into her embrace, but May stiffened, leaned away, her fingers curling into a tight ball like some exotic flower that closed when touched.

Vernie had adored April from the day she was born, and it was easy to love little Junie, but this one ... This was the one she worried about, ached for. She had yet to hear May cry, much less laugh or even smile. She didn't talk when awake, but sometimes muttered in her sleep, and although Vernie struggled to understand, she could make no sense of the soft murmurings. It was like something had been torn out of this middle child. Mostly she sucked on her fingers, caressing her cheek with the rabbit's ears as she watched her sisters with solemn, unblinking eyes. Maybe it came from being the middle one. Maybe from little Junie coming along so soon.

Vernie tried to ignore her weariness as she poured orange juice and settled April at the table with a bowl of instant oatmeal and a slice of toast. She lifted May, limp as a rag doll, onto a chair and fed her from a second bowl of oatmeal. The child was old enough to feed herself; she was old enough to be toilet trained. *But she ain't, so you do what you gotta do and get on with it. Reckon there'll be time for that later.* She poured a handful of Cheerios on the table, hoping that May would at least pick them up and put them into her mouth.

Then to the washing. She stuffed urine-stained sheets and piles of towels into the gaping maw of the washer. She had forgotten how much laundry one child could generate, let alone three—two of them still in diapers and one who wet the bed on a regular basis. The automatic washer and dryer sure made it easier, though. With Mary Ann, she'd had to make do with a wringer washer and a clothesline.

April, trailing crumbs from a slice of toast, sidled into the room. She was filling out some, and yes, the child did seem to remember bits and pieces of those first couple of years in her grandmother's care. Outside, a starling sidestepped along the edge of the birdfeeder. Vernie hoisted the little girl to the top of the dryer. "Looky there, April. Look at that ol' blackbird. He sure thinks he's somethin', don't he?"

April watched in silence for a moment. Then she turned away, a troubled look on her face. "Gran, is black bad?"

"Honey, black ain't bad, and it ain't good, neither. It's just a color. Like red, or green or blue. What made you think it might be bad?"

April popped her fingers in her mouth and didn't answer, but Vernie already knew the answer. She herself remembered the looks, the tone of voice, the hurt of being referred to as *that black girl*.

February melted into a cold and sullen March. Still, the golden haze on the willow tree held promise of the green to come, and the robins were back. In the space of a few weeks, the three little girls had put on weight, their skin had smoothed and softened, and they no longer wore the look of ingrained neglect.

When a sleek black car pulled up in front of the house, Vernie's heart sank. *Gran, is black bad? Oh, lordy, in this case, I'm afraid it is.* The man who might, or might not, be the father of her granddaughters lounged at the wheel, while Mary Ann in knee boots and a leather mini-skirt, her dark hair straightened and dyed a screaming red, climbed out and sashayed up the sidewalk.

April ran to the window, eyes wide. "Gran! It's Mommy! Junie, May, Mommy's here!" Then, she ran to the door, struggling with the stubborn lock. June stood as if hypnotized, nose and both hands pressed against the window. May had scooted into the bedroom, and Vernie guessed she was hiding under the covers or in the closet as she sometimes did.

Mary Ann breezed into the room on a wave of cold air and dropped a cool kiss on her mother's cheek. She hugged April and looked at June, still glued to the window. "Hey, Junie, aren't you going to give Mommy a hug?"

Vernie was torn between joy at seeing her daughter after all this time and fear for her granddaughters. She would have, if she dared, wrapped this hard-faced young woman in her arms and never let go. And she would have, if she could, gathered up the three girls and run so far and fast that they would never be found.

May dashed from the bedroom, her rabbit and a shoe in one hand. Clothing, some hers, some not, spilled from her arms and left a trail behind her as she barreled into Mary Ann. "Mommy, mommy, mommy!" The look on her face was pure bliss.

Mary Ann knelt as best she could in the tight skirt, and gathered her daughters in her arms. "So how's Mommy's little sweethearts? Gran's been spoiling you, I bet." She pried the shoe from May's fist and laid the bundle of clothes on the floor beside her. Her three daughters clung to her, all talking at once. April finally broke away and went to the closet to get her jacket.

"Oh, honey, you can't go with me. You've gotta stay here with Gran. You wouldn't want to leave her here all by herself, would you?" She looked at Vernie. "Bobby has a big business deal brewing in Charleston, so we're headed down there now. We've got a lot of things to get sorted out. Probably won't be back this way for a while. Bobby told me to leave the kids here. You don't mind, do you?"

The horn in the black sports car blared. Mary Ann's head jerked up like a deer spooked on the first day of gun season. "I gotta go."

Six little arms wrapped themselves around her waist and legs. "Mom?" There was both appeal and demand in Mary Ann's voice. Vernie held the children back as Mary Ann opened the door just enough to squeeze through. May broke free and tried to grab onto the leather skirt, but it was too slippery.

April stood at the window waving goodbye, tears streaming down her face. Junie stood beside her, dry-eyed, her face pressed to the window, her hand slowly opening and closing as the car peeled away from the curb. But May threw herself on the floor, kicking and screaming, finally giving vent to all the grief and rage she had kept bottled up during the past weeks. She had been abandoned. Again. "Mommymommymommy!"

Vernie realized now that was the sound she heard at night, a continuous stream of sorrow and loneliness welling up from the child's broken heart. She gathered the kicking, screaming, scratching bundle of hurt to her and settled into the rocking chair. "Shhhh. Shhh, Maysie.

It's all right. Hush now." She bent her head over the child as if to protect her, although she knew she couldn't.

Finally, exhausted, the little girl fell asleep in her arms. Gently, Vernie carried her to the bedroom, tucked the covers around her and placed the rabbit against the tear-streaked cheek.

Vernie's own face was wet as she knelt beside the bed.

Oh, Lord, it's me, your child Vernie . . .

Another Season

At last, at long last, the snow melts, and the season that Rose had feared she might never see comes on fast. Maples blush at the brazen advance, and in the sheltered spots where she planted them all those years ago, hepatica and bloodroot already bloom.

Inside, in the dreary parlor, she watches dust motes slide down shafts of early sunlight, wrinkles her nose at the musty odor of neglect. Once, she would rather have died than let her home get into this condition. But then, she very nearly *had* died. Now, feeling stronger, she itches to get at it, to clean and polish and dust until every trace of the long hard winter is erased. But today there is one last thing she must do for an old friend—something she couldn't do when the wind blew fierce, when under the snow, the ground froze hard as granite.

The stroke, which she suffered last summer, and the months of inactivity have taken their toll. With some difficulty she hobbles to the pantry, removes a basket from the freezer and lifts the lid. Inside an ancient cat lies on a dark paisley cushion, the frozen body curved into a comma. Gently, she touches the stiffened fur, remembers the startling orange color when the cat was young, remembers the incredible softness against her ankles.

"Ah, Mr. Cat," she sighs, "I figured one of us wouldn't make it through the winter, but I never thought it'd be you."

During those dark days, when she battled the lingering effects of her stroke, when she battled her sister Cassie, who was determined to put her away in that awful place—that *lovely facility* as Cassie called it—the old cat never left her side. The fluid motions of youth were long gone for both of them, but when everything seemed hopeless, when she was ready to give in to Cassie's demands, Mr. Cat came to her on arthritic legs, looked at her with those once magnificent tiger eyes, and she knew that she was loved, she was needed. She could hold on a little longer.

Now, tears fill her eyes, and she blows her nose, a loud, uninhibited honk. *Good thing Cassie's not here. She'd figure I was loony for sure.* "So, what was I supposed to do with the poor thing?" she mutters. "Throw him out with the garbage?"

And anyway, what use had she for a freezer? Time was, when her husband Matt was alive, when her son was still home, the freezer was crammed with harvest from the garden—tomatoes and beans and corn, peaches and apples bought at roadside stands, peeled on the broad back porch, and cooked in huge pots on the old fashioned stove until the whole house smelled of summer. Now, only a few frost-covered packages lie forgotten in a drawer that hasn't been opened in years.

"Well," she says, refastening the catch on the basket and slipping her feet into thick-heeled black oxfords. "Well. Might as well get to it."

Below the surface the ground is still frozen. She is soon exhausted, but continues to chop and scrape at the partially frozen earth until her hands are blistered and her breath comes in short gasps. Resting for a moment, she is startled by a husky voice behind her.

"Rushing the season a mite, aren't you?"

She has seen the man before, walking on sunny days, stepping around patches of ice on the cracked and broken sidewalks, swinging his cane in defiance of age and illness and bad weather.

"How's that?" she says.

He stops, bows ever so slightly. "I'm Wesley Preston. Live with my daughter up the street. I was just thinking it seems a bit early for a garden."

She smoothes her pink print housedress, pulls the moth-eaten sweater closer. Realizes that her heavy cotton hose are sagging around her shoe tops.

"Oh!" she stammers, reluctant to speak, for she still has some difficulty with words. "No. No garden." She points to the basket beside her. "My cat."

"I had a cat once. Closer to that cat than I was to my brother, and that's a fact." He looks down at the basket. "What's 'is name?"

"Mr. Cat. Had him for almost seventeen years."

"I called mine Hobo. She was a stray, and you know how it goes. You set out a bowl of milk, and next thing you know, you've got yourself a cat. But . . . my daughter wouldn't let me keep her. Had her put to sleep while I was in the hospital."

"Not very nice," she says slowly, spacing out the words. She likes the way his white hair curls over the collar of his navy sweater, likes the kindness in his faded blue eyes, and suddenly she knows it won't matter if her words don't come out exactly right. "Seems like no one has much use for us, don't it? Reckon they might put *us* to sleep if they dared."

He chuckles, then watches as she digs, seeming to understand that this is something she needs to do herself. He stands with hands folded as she carefully places the basket in the shallow grave, covers it, and pats the soil smooth with her hands. She places a large flat stone over it and wipes her hands on the tail of her sweater. She is sorry she has no flowers, no marker.

She is sorry to see the man go.

Back inside, she puts the kettle on for tea, turns up the fire and warms her hands. Then, invigorated by the fresh air and exercise, she mops and sweeps and dusts and polishes until the fine old wood glows. The carpet and linoleum are dark and worn, but clean. The musty odor of neglect is gone. Rummaging in the sideboard, she finds a fat peach-scented candle still wrapped in yellowed cellophane. She places it on a cracked saucer and holds a match to the wick. The flame wavers and dances in the growing dusk. She stands in the middle of the room, turning slowly, pleased with what she sees—a shabby but neat room, softened and warmed by the glow of candlelight.

In spite of the sadness of saying a final goodbye to Mr. Cat, it's been a good day. Maybe tomorrow she won't wake up, but then again, maybe tomorrow she will bake cookies—soft, chewy oatmeal cookies, heavy with raisins and nuts and spices. And maybe tomorrow, she will invite Mr. Wesley Preston to join her for tea. And why not? Why shouldn't she enjoy the company of an attractive man?

Cassie would laugh. Cassie would tell her to act her age. And maybe she should. Maybe she should just sit down in her chair and wait to die. She's getting old. No, she *is* old; her mirror tells her so. The wrinkled skin, the increasing physical frailty tell her so. But she doesn't feel old. It's as if the years have wrapped themselves around the young Rose, like rings on a tree or the layers of an onion, but she is still there, that other Rose, at the heart of it all.

Outside, spring retreats a few steps as fat lazy snowflakes drift down like a swirl of stars under the streetlight. The snow pleases her, for soon a fluffy white blanket will cover the harsh new grave.

She stands at the window for a long time, marveling at the beauty of snow on tender green leaves. Finally, she closes the curtain, takes off the stern black shoes and lines them up under the chair. Slowly at first, then faster and faster as the years peel away, she glides around the summer-scented room in her stocking feet, moving to the rhythm of a song she had forgotten she ever knew.

Role Model

Old woman—
you, in the yellow dress
and blaze orange sweater,
with a floppy hat tied under your chin
and socks sagging over your shoes—
Do you know how lovely you are?

You don't give a damn for fashion
or what the neighbors think.
You're like a child who hasn't learned—
and doesn't care—
what goes with what,
bold and brazen as a sunrise
that splashes magenta on slate blue
and edges it with peach and crimson and gold.

Come spring you're in your garden,
planting, hoeing, knowing
that soon—surely by June—
you'll pick sugar peas in a chipped blue pan,
spiky green onions freckled with dirt,
and leaf lettuce ruffled as a baby's bonnet.

Old woman,
why is it you never suffered
the angst of my generation?
flower children who left home in psychedelic vans
to search for themselves in communes and cults,
only to return, still searching.
But not you, old woman.
You had no need to find yourself.
You were never lost.

Like A Gift

Old Amos Andersen hadn't been buried a month when Horace Moneypenney came calling on Sally, the grieving widow. Sally had been a plain and simple girl, and now, near seventy, she was a plain and simple woman. Only a fool would have taken the gleam in Horace's eyes for passion. It was greed, pure and simple.

For years now, Horace had coveted the Andersen farm, but Amos, that stubborn old jackass, wouldn't even talk about selling. Except for the rundown service station out on the highway, it was a pretty place. Meadows, laced with a sun-silvered creek, rolled to the mountains on one side and a stand of virgin timber on the other.

The timber alone would bring a nice piece of change, but that wasn't what kept Horace awake nights. There was oil on that land. He could smell it. He could feel the beautiful stuff bubbling under his feet when he paced the boundary. Had he ever been wrong? Never. It was like a gift.

Just last year he had made a killing on the Baxter property—schnookered the old fools out of it, right under the nose of their smart aleck son. Never mind that Case Baxter was a Deputy Sheriff, that he would have inherited the property someday. Never mind that he tailed Horace's sleek black Jaguar all over town, hoping to catch it illegally parked, or going a few miles over the speed limit. Big deal. As if he couldn't afford to pay the fine. The land was now dotted with oil wells, and it was his, all legal. There wasn't a thing anybody could do about it.

Now, I'll have the Andersen place, too, Horace thought, *even if I have to marry it.* He straightened his tie, smoothed his hair, and looked with satisfaction at his reflection in the mirror. *Like taking candy from a baby.*

If you could think of poor, simple Sally as a baby.

"Why, Horace Moneypenney, how neighborly of you to come calling," Sally said as he gingerly made his way up the rickety steps. "Do come in and have a cup of coffee."

Seated on the sway-backed sofa, he took one sip of the nasty stuff and set the cup down. He could hear Sally rummaging in the next room, and soon she appeared, dragging an axe behind her.

"You said at poor Amos's funeral if there was anything you could do—and I know you meant it, Horace, you being an honorable man. Well, as a matter of fact, there is. Winter's coming on, and I haven't a stick of wood." Looking pitiful, she huddled into her threadbare sweater. "There's a whole pile of wood out back, cut, but not split. And I says to myself when I saw you coming up the path, 'There's Horace, bless his heart, come to see what he can do for a poor old widow.'"

Horace looked with distaste at the axe, the skinny wrinkled figure before him, and finally, at the huge pile of wood. Oh, but he wanted that property bad.

Later, hands blistered, he again staggered up the steps. "Sally," he began, "I know it's only been a few weeks since poor Amos's demise, but . . ."

"Oh, you dear man! Look at those blisters! You just sit right down here and let me get you a cup of coffee."

The coffee was even blacker and stronger than before, and Horace's aching body soon persuaded him he was in no shape for either business or romance.

The next visit found him fixing the porch steps, and the one after that, the barn roof. A lesser man might have doubted himself, might have thought that Sally had, somehow, outfoxed him. But not Horace Moneypenney. He knew what he wanted, and he knew how to get it. Patience. That was the key. Patience.

But enough was enough. Tonight, he would either have the land and Sally's hand, or the land and a small dent in his bank account. Thinking of Sally's skinny body and disgusting coffee, he fervently hoped it would be the latter.

"Sally, we have to talk," he said as she met him on the porch.

"You're right, Horace, bless your heart. Come in and have a cup of coffee."

She sloshed the muddy brew into a cup and set it down in front of him. "I've been thinking. It's just not right, me taking advantage of your kindness like this. Truth is, this farm's too much for me, and I know you've wanted it for a long time. All I need is this house and a quarter acre. And because you've been such a good neighbor, I'll do right by you, price-wise."

The figure she named was so low, Horace's eyes bulged in disbelief. Even considering all the blisters and calluses, it was like a gift.

Horace knew all the right people, and he knew how to pull strings. Within a week, he had the deed, crackling like new money, in his pocket. He was a happy man as he parked his car and set off on foot down the rutted road that followed the creek through the woods. He sniffed. It was oil all right. Like a hound tracking a rabbit, he was oblivious to everything but that beautiful perfume.

"Howdy, Horace. Nice piece of property."

Horace recognized that voice. Case Baxter stepped out from behind a tree.

Horace laughed. "Indeed it is. And it's mine, bought and paid for. Not a thing you can do about it."

"Don't plan to," Case said. "What I want to know is, what are *you* gonna do about all this mess?" He gestured to a clearing crowded with rusted barrels.

The alluring aroma had turned acrid. Thick black liquid oozed from several of the barrels and snaked along the ground into the creek. It was oil, all right. Used motor oil. Horace dipped his fingers in another pool and sniffed. Solvent. So that was why Amos wouldn't sell. He was using the farm to dump toxic chemicals from his service station and, from the looks of things, several others as well.

Case leaned against a tree, grinning. "Ugly sight, ain't it? Folks downstream have been complainin'. Dead fish. Stinkin' water. The boys from Washington figure this little ol' crick is polluted clear to the river, and from there, who knows?

"Who would'a thought Amos was such a sly dog? Lucky for him he's dead. Course, it's yours now, all legal. But I wouldn't worry too much, Horace ol' buddy. With the clean-up, fines and a few incidentals, it shouldn't cost you more than a million or so."

Case ambled over and draped a beefy arm across Horace's

shoulder. "Tell you what, ol' buddy. If you find yourself short of cash, I'll take that land that belonged to my folks off your hands. I'd be willing to pay—oh, let's say—what it cost you."

"But . . . but the oil wells . . . " Horace stammered.

"Yeah, they're nasty lookin' things all right, but, hey! We're friends. I'll buy it anyway."

Horace felt cold sweat trickle down his back, dampen his armpits. Somewhere a crow cawed. The creek taunted him, chortling over the oil slick rocks. Or was it Sally, laughing?

Small Shadows, Silent Dreams

Somewhere in the neighborhood a dog barks. The sound, muted and mechanical, drifts through the open window of a third floor bedroom, and Barbara Ann Corley stirs, struggles to free herself from the clinging shell of sleep. She twists her head on the pillow and tries to open her eyes. Cannot. Frightened, she pries the lids apart, lies stiff and straight. Only her eyes move, reaffirming the blue-striped wallpaper, the slanted ceiling, the sun filtering through the white crisscrossed curtains. A breeze moves across her rigid body, and although it is warm for April, she shivers.

She had been dreaming again—the same dream. She walks barefoot along a dark country road. Stones bruise her feet. Huge trees stand shoulder to shoulder, forming an arch overhead. For miles, as far as she can see in any direction, crosses stretch bone white against the blackness. The road goes on and on; it seems to have no beginning and no end.

There is no sound. No breeze stirs the bare branches. No night creature rustles the grass. No sound at all. The night sifts down, heavy and dead. She waits, breathless, but nothing moves. Nothing happens. And always, when the dream is over, her eyes refuse to open, and her body will not move.

Downstairs, a radio plays softly. She moves sluggishly, her muscles still heavy with anticipation. First an arm. Then a leg. Finally she sits on the edge of the bed and rubs the stiffness from her neck. She splashes water on her face in the blue and white bathroom, pulls on jeans and a sweatshirt and stands for a minute at the window, looking at, but not seeing the broad expanse of lawn and the woods beyond. Then she walks slowly down the stairs.

In the kitchen her mother stands at the sink peeling potatoes. "Up so soon?" she asks, looking at the clock. It's after ten. "Well, I guess that's what Saturdays are for. What do you want for breakfast?"

Barbara shrugs.

Her mother dries her hands on a paper towel and moves to the stove. "How about some blueberry pancakes? That's what we had."

The dream, dark and heavy, hovers in the cheerful kitchen. A tumble of hair, copper glinted in the light, hides the girl's face as she traces the swirls in the paisley place mat with her fork. "Did you see her?" she asks. The question has come from deep inside the intricate pattern, and she is surprised.

"What? Did I see who?"

"The baby. Did you see her?"

The woman stands frozen, her back and shoulders rigid. The griddle sizzles and pops. A drop of grease rolls from the poised spatula to the floor. "Yes," she says softly. "Yes, I saw her. She was perfect. Tiny. So tiny. Little toes no bigger than a drop of water. Your daddy could have held her in his hand." Carefully she turns the bubbling batter. "He thought she looked like you, but, of course, she didn't. She didn't look like anybody." For a moment her hand rests on the slack muscles of her belly.

It is quiet in the sunny kitchen. Grease sputters on the griddle. A plate of steaming pancakes slides across the polished table. Barbara picks at the crisp golden crust and remembers that day early last summer.

It was the last day of school, her last day of junior high. She came around the sidewalk, excited and a little sad. Her denim backpack, heavy with dirty gym clothes and books and papers, dangled from one shoulder.

Her mother sat on the picnic bench in her best dress, her legs stretched out in front of her. She cradled a cup of coffee in her hands. Barbara looked at the legs in the unaccustomed hose and high heels and knew something was wrong. She stood silent, shifting from one foot to the other.

Her mother was looking at something beyond her left shoe. "I'm pregnant," she said.

Barbara stood very still.

Then her mother looked straight at her. There were tears in her eyes. "I'm pregnant," she said bitterly.

"You're what? You can't be pregnant," Barbara said. "You're..." She almost said *too old*. "You're not sure, are you? Maybe it's something else. Maybe it's a mistake."

The woman was crying in earnest now, mascaraed tears streaming down her face. "No mistake. I've just come from the doctor." Coffee sloshed across the flowered print of her dress as she opened her arms to the trembling girl.

Shocked and embarrassed, Barbara backed away. "You could have an abortion," she blurted.

The woman closed her eyes and shook her head.

"Why not? Lots of women do."

"Oh, honey, how could I? I look at you—so beautiful, so grown up. You were once no more than this." Eyes brimming with tears, the woman touched her flat stomach with the tips of her fingers. "I remember how you looked, how you felt. I remember how you smelled, all milky and sweet. I remember the silly, satisfied look on your face while you were nursing. I couldn't. I never could."

Barbara watched a tiny caterpillar inch its way across the redwood table. "Does Daddy know?"

The woman nodded.

"And?"

"Oh, he thinks it's wonderful. Why wouldn't he?" Her voice held a touch of sarcasm. "He always wanted another child." There was a long pause, and her voice softened. "*I* wanted another child. But now... Barbie, you're almost fifteen! Some of my friends are having grandchildren. How can I start all over again? How can I?"

For an instant brown eyes met brown eyes. Then Barbara turned and ran into the house, ran to her room and locked the door. She dropped the backpack, gave it a vicious kick. A tennis shoe bounced to the floor. She picked it up and heaved it against the closet door.

The months passed. June... July... August. Once reconciled to the pregnancy, Barbara's mother became obsessed with it, or so it seemed to Barbara. She followed to the letter her doctor's instructions on diet and rest and exercise. She studied breast feeding and Lamaze; books and pamphlets were everywhere: on the bedside stand, in the kitchen, on the coffee table. She wore shapeless tops and a soft secret smile. It seemed to Barbara that every conversation was about the pregnancy or the baby. She felt as if she were on a tiny raft, drifting farther and farther away from home, from all that was familiar.

Her father wore a foolish grin from daylight to dark. He whistled tunelessly as he papered and painted Barbara's new bedroom and bath on the third floor. "A suite for my sweetie," he said. Her old room, painted a buttery yellow and furnished in white wicker, became a nursery.

The new blue and white room with its virginal ruffles, its slanted ceiling and dormer windows, revolted her. The fields and roadsides, exploding with life—groundhogs and birds and rabbits and flowers—revolted her. Her mother's swollen breasts and belly and ankles, her father's sappy good humor, revolted her.

She watched them, her mother and father, saw their secret smiles, the new intimate way they touched. At night their whispers drifted up to her through the heating vent, until finally she buried her head in the pillow and slept.

Did they try to draw her into that magic circle? Yes, she supposed they did. Her mother dangled the lure of soft pastel garments and cuddly stuffed animals, rattles and cunning mobiles. "See what your gramma sent," she would say . . . or, "Look what I found on sale."

Secretly, Barbara visited the waiting nursery often. She sorted the blankets and booties and sleepers, held the tiny undershirts aloft on her palm, doubting that anything human could possibly fit into something so small.

Her father, too, tried to tempt her with broad winks and exaggerated groans as he helped her mother heave her bulk into and out of chairs. She remembers his soft chuckle as the taut mound rippled under his big hand. "Come here, Barbie," he would say. "You've got to feel this!" But always she turned away, retreated to her room or to the friendly woods that separated their property from the mountains beyond.

September came and Barbara went to the big new high school. It seemed she was always lost and always late. She was too embarrassed to face her friends, tried to avoid them, but on the third day they caught up with her in the restroom.

"Hey, Barb," Megan said, lipsticking her round mouth. "I hear your mom's pregnant."

Barbara felt her face grow hot. "So? Who told you?"

"Now really, Barbara, it's not exactly something you have to be *told*," giggled Cheryl, curving her hands several inches in front of her stomach. "My mom saw her at Krogers and she said she's big as a barn."

Barbara felt sick. "I've got to get to class."

Their words followed her into the hall. "Can you imagine? At her age! Really gross!"

October passed in a flurry of blue skies and brilliant leaves. The anticipation grew until the house seemed to vibrate with it. Then suddenly, the first week in November, it ended. Anxious voices in the night. A flurry of drawers and doors opening and closing. Hurried goodbyes. Silence. She was alone in the house, in the blue and white bedroom. She watched the numbers on the digital clock . . . 2:12; 2:35; 3:01. She dozed, awoke, watched the clock. Finally, just as the new day was insinuating itself into the room, she awoke from her fitful sleep to find her father bending over her. His face was lined and streaked with tears. Her hand went to her mouth. Her eyes, heavy with sleep and dread, asked the question.

"Your mother's all right," he said. "But the baby . . ." His voice broke. "Oh, Barbie, she didn't make it." Awkwardly he gathered her to him, and she could feel his tears dampening her hair.

The door to the yellow room was closed. The baby bed was taken down; the tiny garments disappeared. The box of Pampers, forgotten in the closet, remained unopened. There were no bottles in the sink, no cries in the night. Nothing had changed. It was just as it had always been.

Thanksgiving and Christmas came and went. January passed, then February and March. She was never mentioned, that wee intruder. Her brief existence was never acknowledged until this morning when the question came twisting up from the convoluted whorls of the paisley place mat.

"Did you see her?"

The potato peelings slide silently into the sink. The woman's shoulders are curiously rounded, as if the bone beneath has begun to melt.

The capsule of grief and guilt dissolves, and Barbara hides her face in her hands. "Oh, Mom, I'm sorry! I'm so sorry!"

The woman crosses the kitchen, loops the gleaming hair in her hand. She presses her own wet cheek against her daughter's, and together they cry.

"I would have loved her, Mom. I *wanted* to love her. I didn't want her to die!"

"I know," she croons, rocking her daughter back and forth. "I know." The woman sits down, drops her clasped hands between her knees. She is looking at Barbara, but she sees something inside herself. "I never held her," she says softly. "We didn't even name her. I wish we had. I wish I had held her just once."

She is silent, lost in thought, as Barbara opens the door and steps into the bright spring morning.

The girl has no clear idea where she is going as she wheels her bike from the garage and pedals aimlessly down Oak Ridge Road. At the corner, an adolescent Dalmatian, all spots and feet and tail, bounces toward her, inviting a game of tag. She stops, scratches the dog behind the ear. "Hi, there ol' Sparky-spark. You woke me up this morning, didn't you? And what are you doing in the road? You go on home now." She gives the dog a final pat and pedals off.

She turns left, then left again. She feels the sting of wind in her face, smells the damp earthy perfume of spring. She is acutely aware of the still new breasts and waist and hips, of the blood pounding through her veins. She is alive. She's alive, and that tiny threat, her almost sister, is dead.

"She didn't make it," her father had said. "She didn't make it."

Again, she remembers the unexpected flare of relief, and again she is seared by shame and remorse.

"I'm sorry I'm sorry I'm sorry!" she sobs. "I'm sorry."

The bike spurts across a two-lane highway, through massive stone gates. It wobbles dangerously, and she realizes she is on a rough graveled path. Giant trees stand against the sky. The little white cross stands at the top of a rise, just as she remembers it.

The small oblong is covered with new grass and a sprinkling of white violets. She kneels and brushes the dirt away from the marker. *BABY GIRL CORLEY*, it says. The ground is wet and cold through the knees of her jeans. "I'm sorry, baby," she whispers. "I didn't want you to die."

A sudden breeze lifts her hair, fingers her neck, dries the dampness between her shoulder blades. She studies the plain white cross, the anonymous marker. "Poor little Baby No Name," she sighs.

Sunlight streaks through clouds, now piled high on the horizon. It strikes the cross, casts a small shadow across the violet-studded grass. The shadow lengthens, touches the girl briefly. Then it is gone.

Voice Of The Dove

Eve first saw the girl on a Tuesday. Standing at the kitchen window, she watched her slog through the mud and slush on Mill Creek Road. Then, minutes later, she came back, eyes straight ahead, steps precise, almost as if she were marching. Even from her distant vantage point, Eve could see there was not much more than skin and bone beneath what appeared to be a khaki poncho or cape.

Strangers in these parts were rare, and it had been weeks since Eve had seen another human being. Record snows that winter covered the narrow windows and blocked the doors of the hundred-year-old farm house. Mason, damn him, disappeared right after Thanksgiving, and she, pregnant and alone in this God-forsaken place, was trapped inside for days at a time. Cows with milk-heavy udders bawled in the barn. The rabbits, poor things, froze in their hutch. She thought spring would never come.

It did, of course, though reluctantly, cold and damp. She felt it trickling through her veins like snow melt from the mountain. Eve longed to call out to the girl, but something in the fierce concentration stopped her. She watched until the figure disappeared, then set to work skinning the rabbits like Mason had taught her.

She imagined his shoulder warm and solid against her, his hands guiding hers as she made a horizontal cut across the back. The flesh was slick and cold as she worked her fingers under the matted fur to loosen it. Like stripping wet pajamas from a child, she thought as she peeled the top half inside out toward the heads, the lower portion over the hind legs. By the time the rabbits were gutted and soaking in a bowl of salt water, her hands were as red and raw as the hurt inside.

Where her husband had gone, or precisely why, Eve didn't know, but gone he was. She had kissed him, then watched him drive away that day in the old blue Ford. He didn't look back, she remembered later, didn't wave as he usually did. Then truck and driver were lost in the purple haze of Indian summer.

Supper that night grew cold on the table, and dusk became full dark. A sliver of moon was framed in the kitchen window, as reluctantly, she dialed her mother-in-law. Eve tucked a strand of hair behind her ear as the phone rang once, twice, three times. She pictured the pinched little woman taking a long drag on her cigarette, squinting into the smoke as the phone rang a fourth time. The voice that answered was raspy with nicotine and irritation.

"Hello, Mother Davis," Eve said, twisting the cord around her finger, dreading the question she had to ask. "Mason's a little late getting home, and I was wondering if he might have stopped off there?"

The woman laughed. "What's the matter, Evie? Lose track of him, did ya? I warned you, girlie. Remember? Mason ain't one to be tied down—leastways, not for long."

Oh, Eve had heard the sly remarks behind cupped hands. *Mason had a way with the women*, they said. *And why would old Mason settle for skinny little Evie when there were so many willing to lift their skirts for him?*

She had been a fool to think that Mason, the man she had adored since she was fourteen, could ever love her as she loved him. In a way, she had been expecting him to go, wondered each time he drove away if he would be back.

As darkness deepened, the surrounding mountains seemed to close in on the old house. Finally, near panic, she dialed the sheriff. "Buck ain't here, Evie," Clara, the sheriff's wife said. "Away on official business."

Eve suspected the *official business* was a coon hunt.

"Don't you worry none now, dearie. That's just the way men are. Sometimes they just gotta get away, especially when they first hear a young'un's on the way. He'll be back. You'll see."

But he didn't come back, and by the time the sheriff's four-wheel drive skidded into the yard the next afternoon, Indian summer was buried in a foot of snow.

And so, just like that, Mason left her. Took off without a word. During the short gray-white days, watching the snow drift higher and higher, she cursed him, hated him. But at night, buried in quilts, she remembered the sound of his voice as he whispered her name, remembered the warmth of him, the weight of his body. Remembered how he filled her until she was empty of all but love.

Now, in early April, the ice and snow had shrunk to islands in a sea of mud that sucked at her boots as she trudged from the barn to the broad porch, a pail of milk in each hand. A fine rain misted her hair, and she wrinkled her nose at the wet-dog smell of Mason's old mackinaw.

In the still bare walnut tree, a pair of doves fluttered, awkwardly attempting to mate. She had heard, or thought she did, their mournful call all during those dark winter days. "Stupidest birds I ever saw," she muttered, remembering how they fouled the porch, how every spring they tried to build nests in the eave troughs.

She set the pails on the porch, absently caressing the mound of her stomach where the seed Mason had planted, then abandoned, grew. She gazed out over the pastel-tinged trees to the road that snaked down the mountain to Mill Creek. It made no sense after all this time, but she still expected to see the flash of blue through the trees. It was then she saw the girl for the second time.

"Hello," Eve called through cupped hands, but the girl didn't stop, didn't turn. Gave no sign she had heard. Desperate for the sound of a human voice, Eve ran to the road, slipping and sliding on patches of ice. But the girl had disappeared.

On the third day, the misty rain became a downpour, but like before, the thin figure appeared, looking neither left nor right, splashing through ankle-deep puddles as if they weren't there. Eve grabbed a slicker and ran to the road just in time to see her make a sharp turn and come back toward her. As she drew closer, Eve could see her lips moving, as if she were counting her steps.

"Hello there," Eve said, smiling. "Bad day to be out." But the figure didn't break her deliberate stride. Eve stepped in front of her. She could see now that it wasn't a girl, but a middle-aged woman. Matted hair funneled water into the pinched face. An old army blanket covered the stick figure, and eyes, dark and frightened, darted side to side, seeking escape.

"Hey," Eve said softly, "don't be afraid. I won't hurt you." Bird-claw hands worried the tattered blanket. Eve touched the soaked wool lightly. The woman trembled but did not draw away.

"It's nice and warm inside," Eve said, pointing to the lighted window. "Why don't you come in for a few minutes?"

The woman remained silent. Then, looking at Eve for the first time, she whispered. "I saw something."

"You saw something? What did you see?"

The eyes again darted away. "Something." She began marching in place, silently counting her steps. "Walk like this. Make it go away."

"You're shivering. Come on up to the house and get warm. Please. I'll fix you something warm to drink."

The woman smiled slyly and licked her lips. "You got any cocoa? I like cocoa."

Back inside, Eve wrung the blanket out as best she could, hung it by the stove, then put a pan of milk on to heat. She mixed cocoa and sugar in a small bowl and stirred it in. "I've seen you on the road a couple of times," she said over her shoulder. "Where do you live?"

The woman didn't answer for a long time. Then, "Down there," she muttered without looking up.

"Down where?"

Eyes open wide, the woman stared into space. "I saw something down there," she said.

"Can't you tell me what it was?" Eve prodded, but there was no answer. The smell of wet wool and hot cocoa permeated the room. "What's your name?" Eve asked gently as she placed a steaming cup in the chapped hands.

The woman gulped the scalding liquid and held out the cup for more. "Mostly folks just call me *You*." Her voice was rough, the laugh as musical as a child's. "But I calls me Adah."

"Well, Adah, I've made a good rabbit stew for supper. You'd be doing me a favor if you'd stay."

The stew was thick, savory with onions and carrots and potatoes and celery, and the woman ate as if she were starved, which, Eve realized, she very nearly was. Later, Adah curled up like a cat on the rug by the fire and went to sleep.

The rain stopped sometime during the night. At daybreak, Eve heard a rustling in the kitchen and found Adah trying to hide the rest of the stew, the tin of cocoa and a loaf of bread under the still damp blanket.

"It's all right, Adah. You're welcome to what's left. Are you going home now?"

The dark eyes turned inward, as if seeing some private terror.

Eve touched her shoulder. "Tell me what you're afraid of Adah. Maybe I can help."

Without a word, the bony hand closed on Eve's arm, drawing her out the door, into the fresh-washed morning. Adah marched to the road, down the mountain, her grip tightening as they neared a sharp turn.

On a slight rise, an abandoned one-room school overlooked a steep gully. *My God*, Eve thought, eyeing the broken windows, *she must have been there all winter*! Several times, she had seen smoke rising from that direction.

Adah stopped abruptly, her fingers digging into Eve's arm now. "Down there," she whispered. "I had a mind to hunt me a mess of creasy greens, and I saw something down there."

Eve stepped off the road onto the shoulder where two deep ruts cut across the steep drop off. There at the bottom of the ravine, still partially buried in snow, she saw chunks of blue metal. A boot. Chrome. Broken glass, catching and throwing back the morning sun. And amid the scattered wreckage, scraps of red and black plaid. She knew that fabric—flannel it was, soft and warm. She had washed it, hung it to dry. She had rested her cheek against it, the beat of her husband's heart strong in her ear.

Adah whimpered. "Go away. Make it go away."

Eve stumbled back to the road. *Oh, God, oh, God!* She ran and fell, ran and fell. Adah followed at her heels.

Early that afternoon, Eve's water broke. The baby, a girl, was stillborn. Adah, crooning tunelessly, wrapped the tiny body in the rough woolen blanket. "I had me a baby once," she said, gently rocking the bundle in her arms. "Her name was Annie Laurie."

Eve closed her eyes and turned her face to the wall, seeing only the naked, bloody bodies of the rabbits. She passed a hand over her eyes and wondered why there were no tears, no wails of anguish.

She remembered nothing of the weeks that followed. Mason had left her for good, and she knew now that spring indeed would never come. But the days warmed, and in the shaded valleys, snow gave way to wild flowers. The bulbs she had planted in October bloomed red and yellow and purple against the greening grass. Their bright colors were an affront, for inside, deep in the hidden places, the ice remained, untouched by sunshine or bird song or the scent of hyacinths.

She bumbled through the days like a sleepwalker, doing for the second time chores she had just finished. Time and again she saw the glimmer of blue through tender new leaves, but it was only the sky. She heard the rattle of the old truck in the cacophony of night sounds, dreamed of naked rabbits, and tiny, still babies named Annie Laurie. Rising at dawn, she wrapped herself in layers of clothing and sat shivering before a roaring fire that did not warm her.

Adah still walked the road every day, but her curious marching had stopped. Thanks to the bounty of Eve's cellar, she had grown less gaunt and more lucid. Day after day she came, silent and without complaint, to the sweltering house. She washed and cooked and cleaned, patted Eve's hand, brushed her hair, gave what comfort she could.

Standing at the kitchen window, staring listlessly at nothing in particular, Eve saw her amble from the road onto the lane that led to the house. In a bright pink dress that Eve had given her, a blaze orange hunting jacket, and a yellow straw hat with faded red flowers, she looked like a hundred pounds of sunrise that had slipped its moorings and settled to earth. Every few yards, she stopped, head back, mouth open, and slowly turned around. What she was looking at—bird or plane or cloud—only Adah knew.

"Come here!" she yelled, spying Eve at the window. "I see something!"

I see something. Eve felt the coldness expand, crowding bile into her throat. Pulling on another sweater, she stepped into the sunshine. With one hand Adah squashed the garish hat tight to her head. The other pointed to the roof. "Look!" she cried as a dove settled into the eave trough.

Eve shaded her eyes with her hand. "It's got a nest up there," she said. "The damned thing's got a nest up there!" It had been a long time since she felt anything, but now a fine rage grew in her as she dragged a stool from the kitchen.

"Stupid bird," she muttered. The stool tilted as the legs sunk into the soft dirt around the peonies. Standing on tiptoe on the second step, she caught her breath and steadied herself against the downspout. She liked her feet, both of them, on the ground. "Damned birds. Clog the gutter and I'll have a cellar full of water." Her voice grew louder as she jabbed viciously at the mass. This was Mason's job. Why wasn't he here to do it?

From the fence the doves cooed softly, watching with unblinking eyes the destruction of their nest. "Stupid birds don't know ... don't even *care* if your babies drown."

She flipped another wad of dead grass and twigs and green growing things to the ground. She was crying now, a hot river coursing up from some hurt, hidden place. Kneeling, she raked the debris from the flowerbed. Then she saw it, a fragile white oval. The egg was still warm. She cupped it in her hands, clear plasma leaking through her fingers. "Oh," she moaned. "Ohhh. They're dead, Adah. They're dead."

"Don't cry," Adah said, plopping down beside her to study the egg. "That old mama bird, she'll be back. Soon as we're gone, she'll be back."

Eve sobbed and the birds sat on the fence, waiting. Finally, exhausted, she leaned into Adah's arms. The sun, insistent as a lover, warmed her, and under the ice, she felt the first faint stirring. She raised her face to its heat, breathed it in great shuddering gulps, until at last, winter lost its grip. With the thaw came an aching tingle. She recognized what had been there all along, buried under the grief and anger. Mason didn't leave her willingly. He loved her. And yes, spring *would* come this year, and next year, and every year after that. The flash of blue through the trees was only sky, would always be only sky, and the night sounds only insects searching for a mate, or the rustle of animals as they foraged for food.

The wind, bearing a soft subtle fragrance, stirred tender new leaves, and the song of a bird she could not name rose above the mournful cry of the doves. Rocking back on her heels, Eve scooped a depression in the soft dirt and lined it with the remnants of the nest. Then, carefully, gently, she placed the broken egg inside and covered it with the rich spring earth.

After Supper
(For Terrye)

Remember the primroses?
my daughter says, as ice
melts in our glasses
and cicadas reel in the day.

Yes. The primroses.
I'd forgotten
how we gathered at dusk
to watch them bloom—
you and the boys in pajamas
bare feet in dew-wet grass
mosquitoes buzzing in our ears.

We held our breath as petals
turned in slow pirouette,
yellow parasols unfurled
luminous as moons,
one, then another and another,
like time lapse photography.

They're gone now;
the garden too.
But you beckon and I follow
to your garden where primroses
like cupped hands
catch dew
and starlight
and summer.

In Mysterious Ways

The TV was on. Robert and Karen sprawled on opposite ends of the couch, waiting out the string of commercials for cat food, feminine protection, toothpaste and paper towels. Five-year-old Ellen lay on the floor coloring, while Bobby, just past two, tugged the long braid that hung down his sister's back, and then, under cover of that diversion, snatched her crayons.

They were beautiful children—rosy cheeked, brown-eyed blondes. Not long ago, Robert and Karen would have separated them, smiled at each other and congratulated themselves on making such exquisite babies. Then the expanse of slip-covered couch between them would have disappeared, and the kids would have been put to bed early.

Now, commercials over, a woman with thick glasses and long red fingernails gestured dramatically. "There was this bright—actually this blinding—light, and the next thing I knew, I was on a table, the ... bleep bleep ... coldest piece of metal you could ever imagine, and these ... these things with huge heads and bodies that were like ... ummm ... kinda like lava lamps, ya know, were standing around me, sticking things, probes, I guess you would call them, into my body, but I couldn't feel a thing."

"Now, Susan—may I call you Susan?" a man, with hair too perfect to be real, said. "You're telling us—you expect us to believe— you were taken up in a spaceship and examined by *aliens*?"

"What a bunch of crap," Robert said, switching channels.

"Ummm," Karen replied. "I went to school with that girl. She always was a little ... different."

"Know what?" Robert said, reaching across the cushion to tap her on the knee. "I think we need to get away for a few days, all four of us. Why don't we spend Easter weekend at the cabin?"

The log cabin, rustic and remote, had been in Robert's family for generations. It perched in a clearing at the top of a hill, overlooking rolling fields of broom sage and second growth woodland. The nearest neighbor was more than two miles away. It wasn't Karen's idea of a fun weekend, but they *did* need to get away, and there was no money for a real vacation. Unconsciously, she looked at Bobby.

"He'll be fine," Robert said.

He'll be fine. How many times had she repeated that to herself these last few months? Bobby *looked* fine. Most of the time, he *seemed* fine, but the truth was, he wasn't fine.

Most mothers would not have thought of Bobby as a sickly child, but he was never completely well. Nothing really serious, but as one illness morphed into another, Karen knew something was wrong. "He's fine," doctor after doctor pronounced. "You worry too much, Mother," said another. Finally, probably tired of Karen's nagging, they were referred to a specialist. Hours in waiting rooms with a fretful toddler. Weeks of tests. Days waiting for results. Finally, an answer. Primary immune deficiency.

"AIDS?" Karen whispered.

The doctor shook his head. "No. AIDS is acquired. This is genetic, usually mother to son."

Mother to son? The words expanded and blurred, ran together until they filled her head. *My baby! Oh my God, what have I done to my baby?*

Karen hadn't been to church since she was a child, and if she had ever known how to pray, she had long since forgotten. Yet, as she peeled potatoes, as she washed the piles of socks and underwear and sheets and towels, as she reached into the mailbox for the daily raft of bills, she found herself saying over and over, *Please, God, please.* Please what? Please heal my child? Please take away this guilt, this awful pain? Please make things right between Robert and me? *Please God . . .*

Easter came late that year, and it was warm, almost too warm, as they packed the station wagon Good Friday morning. Cato, a shaggy mutt with huge feet and an enthusiastic tail, raced in excited circles, yapping and nipping the seat of Bobby's pants when he wandered too close to the street.

Ellen stood, toes pointed in, one arm raised as if she were holding someone's hand.

"Let's leave Elliott at home," Karen said.

"Can't." Ellen shook her head and popped her fingers into her mouth. "He'll get lonesome. And scared."

Elliott had appeared while Robert and Karen were shuttling from one doctor to another, searching for an answer to Bobby's various illnesses. Ellen insisted she had found him, all alone and scared, hiding under the porch at Grandma Scott's. Karen wasn't sure her daughter's attachment to the imaginary playmate was healthy, but she had done little to discourage it. She was, in fact, grateful for the comfort her little girl drew from her silent friend.

And so, with Elliott safely settled on top of the ice chest, they set off for the cabin. Within minutes, Bobby, clutching a handful of Cato's fur, was asleep. Reaching over the back of the seat, Karen covered the small hand with her own, as if to hide the bruise left by his latest transfusion.

"You may not think so now," the doctor had said, "but you *can* learn to live with this."

Robert squeezed Karen's hand as the doctor went on. "There are treatments. But you'll need to keep him out of crowds and away from other children. If there's a bug out there, Bobby's going to get it."

Maybe it won't be so bad after all, Karen thought. But that was before that first treatment, before the sight of her baby, strapped down, helpless, yet screaming and reaching for her with his eyes as the needle was threaded into his tiny vein.

By the time they reached the farm, it was well past noon, and both children were hungry and cranky. While Robert unpacked the wagon, she slapped peanut butter on two pieces of bread, cut an apple in two, poured two plastic glasses of milk, and settled the children at a rickety card table to eat. Afterwards, with only token resistance, they curled up on opposite ends of the musty cot for a nap.

Outside, Robert, whistling softly through his teeth, strung a line between two trees for the inevitable wet towels and tee shirts. Easing the screen door shut behind her, Karen crossed the porch and sat down on the top step. The sun warmed her as her ears filled with the country quiet and her nose with the scent of new growth. The soft colors of crabapple and redbud and dogwood and tender green leaves wound through the woods like a pastel scarf. Clouds, gentle as angel wings, drifted across the sky. The pain receded. For those few minutes at least, she was at peace.

That evening, she heated chili on the Coleman stove, and later, they all sat on the porch, huddled together under blankets, watching as the moon and stars possessed the endless expanse of sky. The children were soon asleep, and she and Robert, tired and happier than they had been for months, crawled into their sleeping bags and slept soundly.

Morning came, and while coffee perked on the stove, they zipped into hooded sweatshirts and, with Bobby perched high on Robert's shoulders, waded through the wet grass, over a once-upon-a-time fence, into a field where, years ago, cattle had been pastured. Streamers of mist hung in the trees and lay in the hollows like newborn lakes.

Suddenly Robert stopped and whispered, "Cato! Stay!" Turning, he put his finger to his lips. There, not twenty yards away, stood a doe with twin fawns. The two families stared at each other. Then the deer, white tails high, bounded away.

During lunch, Ellen announced that Elliott wanted a wiener roast—with marshmallows. So at six o'clock, with the sun melting into the trees behind the cabin, Karen stood at the window, chopping an onion, watching Robert chop wood. He was shirtless and sweaty, his face streaked with dirt, and for the first time in a very long time, she felt a throb of delicious, licentious lust.

"What did we do with the matches?" he said from the doorway.

"Come over here and I'll show you," she said.

Just then, Ellen appeared at the door. "Where's your brother?" they asked at the same time.

"Right there with Cato," the little girl replied, pointing to a space directly in front of the window.

The clearing was empty. Romance forgotten, they bumped each other through the narrow doorway.

"Bobby! Cato! Cato, here boy! Come on, boy."

They looked all through the cabin, around the cabin, in the margin of trees at the foot of the hill.

"He was right there when I came in. He couldn't have gotten far." Robert put two fingers in his mouth and gave a shrill whistle. There was no answer. Even the rustling grass and the restless trees had grown still.

"My God, Robert, it's getting dark! Do something!"

"Wherever he is, Cato's with him. He'll be all right. You run down to the road and see if you can find some help. I'll take the wagon and drive through the field. Maybe he went back to find the deer."

Karen grabbed Ellen's hand, but the child pulled away, protesting. "Elliott..."

"Forget Elliott. Come on!"

The road was empty. No one to help. No Cato. No little boy.

"Here, Cato. Here, boy. Bobby! Answer me! Where are you?"

Night was coming on fast now. Soon it would be dark. Dragging the sobbing Ellen, gasping for breath, Karen ran back up the hill to the cabin just as the headlights of the station wagon topped the hill from the other direction. Robert had found him; she knew he had. But when Robert opened the door, he was alone.

She stood crying, gripping Ellen's hand so tightly that the child cried out. Karen didn't know what to do next. Then, through the open door of the cabin, she heard a low growl. Cato!

Bobby, pale and trembling, lay on the cot sucking his thumb. Cato cowered on the floor, fur bristling, a continuous low growl rumbling in his throat.

Karen scooped the boy into her arms while Robert encircled them both. "What happened, sweetheart? Where did you go? Mommy and Daddy were scared to death."

"I was scared, too," Ellen, forgotten and forlorn, sobbed.

Karen drew her frightened daughter into the circle and dropped a kiss on top of her head. "Of course, you were, honey. But everything's okay now. See? Bobby's fine."

"Bobby-boy, don't you ever do that to us again," Robert said, and for an instant Karen thought he might shake the child. "We looked everywhere. Where were you?"

Bobby rolled his brown eyes to the rafters and pointed a small finger. "Up," he said. "Up. Waaay up." Cato crouched beside him, then, head and tail down, the dog crept into the farthest corner of the cabin.

Robert and Karen looked up, into the exposed beams, knowing there was no way for a two-year old to get *up*.

"Stubborn little brat," Robert grinned. "You're not going to tell us, are you?"

On the first Monday in May, at exactly 10:43 a.m. by the clock on the microwave, the phone rang. Later, Karen realized that she did not cringe, did not hesitate to answer that infernal bearer of bad news, as she usually did.

"Karen, Bobby's tests are back." Dr. Douglas was on the speakerphone, and Karen imagined that God would sound just like that, only louder. "We can't explain it, but he's completely normal."

"Are you sure?" she whispered.

"I'm sure. There's nothing wrong with Bobby." The doctor's voice was firm. "What can I say? When you've been in this business as long as I have, you learn to believe in miracles."

Karen raised her hand skyward. *Thank You, God!*

There was a celebration that day, and all the mothers in the neighborhood brought their kids for cake and Kool-Aid—and if the kids brought along a few germs, well, that's the way it was with kids. It wasn't a matter of life and death.

And miles away, just beyond the remote field where they had watched the deer that Easter Saturday morning, a circle of earth, recently scorched and bare, was already covered with new grass.

Shadow Of The Mountain

"That old mountain, she always be there," Aunt Esta would say when she got in one of her moods. "She be there before you, before me. 'Fore anybody, I reckon, 'cept maybe God." Then she'd laugh, an explosive snort, before she rambled on. "Just sets there. Don't do nothin' but set there, like a big ol' spider."

Her hand on my shoulder was as thin and crooked as the ginseng drying in the corner, as we watched shadow ooze across the long narrow valley and up the mountains to the west. "See that shadow? That be her web. It reach out and catch everything it touch." She nipped my cheek with fingers that had no more life than the dried turkey bones strung across the open window. "Mark my words, missy, she catch you, too." And then she'd look up at the mountain like she saw Moses descending, nod her head and go back to her rocking.

I was fourteen or fifteen then, counting down the years until I graduated from Eastland High and could leave the valley. *Not me,* I thought. *That old mountain won't get me.*

The day after graduation, I packed my few belongings in a cardboard dress box, tied it with string and set out down the dirt track to seek my fortune, just like in the fairy tales. I looked back only once. Aunt Esta stood in the middle of the lane, her arms crossed over her chest as if trying to hold on to me a little longer, but I didn't turn back, didn't even wave.

I could have waved at least. She was the only family I had. One night when I was about nine months old, a truck full of young couples coming home from a shivaree missed a curve on the narrow mountain road. Five people, including my parents, were killed. Aunt Esta wasn't a blood relative; she was a neighbor who had offered to tend me that evening, and since no one else claimed me, she did. She was old even then, a widow with no child of her own, and I must have been a burden.

But I didn't think about that then. I just hurried on down that road, away from the mountain, away from Aunt Esta. Dust rose around me in little puffs, etching the pattern of sandal straps on my feet. By the time I reached the hard road, I must have been a sorry sight. Cars and trucks whizzed by, going . . . *Where?* I wondered.

By mid-morning, I was hot and tired and thirsty. When an old station wagon screeched to a stop and backed up, I didn't ask questions, even though it appeared to be held together with baling wire and bumper stickers. Hand-painted red letters, spelling out *Caledonia Free-Will Church*, staggered along the side. Children of all ages and descriptions hung out of every window and over the tailgate.

The Rev. Mr. McIvor was ruddy and good-natured, with a laugh that boiled up like syrup in a pot. His wife, a tiny, quiet woman with a sweet smile, held an infant on her lap and shifted a toddler closer to make room for me. Not all the children, I learned, were theirs. Some were orphans that the McIvors had taken in; others came for church school on Sundays and stayed. I finally gave up trying to sort them out.

From the first, I was part of it, the big, chaotic household. Mama (I never heard her called anything else) scurried around from early morning to late night, feeding babies and settling arguments and wiping noses. I trailed after her, kissing hurts and wiping tears she had missed. Sometimes, on cool summer mornings as I picked dewy greens from the garden, or during the long evenings as we gathered for vespers on the broad porch, I imagined I could see the mountain in the distance, its shadow, like tentacles, lengthening, reaching out for me.

Still, I was happy there. Then Jeremy Campbell appeared at the door, looking for odd jobs. Mama took him in, fed him, and like me, he stayed. He had the darkest hair and the bluest eyes I had ever seen. For me, at least, it was love at first sight. We were inseparable, stealing kisses and hurried love whenever and wherever we could. Before long, nature took its course.

One evening after supper I drew him outside, into the early autumn darkness, to share my wonderful secret. The next morning, he wolfed down Mama's breakfast of eggs and grits and biscuits without looking at me. By lunchtime, he was gone. I never heard from him again.

Jessica was born in June in the McIvor's crowded bedroom. She was a miracle of soft black curls and pink skin and blue, blue eyes, and I loved her so much it was like a hurt that never went away. In the mornings when she woke with a mewling little cry, I took her into my bed, nuzzling her sweetness as she nursed, and it was on such a morning that the dreams began.

Aunt Esta, sick. Aunt Esta calling me, needing me. Aunt Esta dead. So it wasn't the mountain reaching out for me; it was those old turkey bone fingers, pulling, pulling me back.

What I felt for Aunt Esta was the other side of the love I had for my baby. It was grudging, unwilling, owed. But it was love, nevertheless. I had to go back.

Aunt Esta wasn't sick, not physically anyway, and she certainly wasn't dead. She met me as I came struggling back up the same road I had left on, little Jessica riding low on my hip.

Just like that old mountain, I thought. *Aunt Esta will always be here.*

"Well," she said, looking from me to the wriggling bundle I carried. She wiped her hands on her apron and took Jessica from me. "Well . . . It happens. Reckon it had to happen. No daddy, no brothers. No way of knowin' the ways of a man. You was ripe for the pickin'."

Inside, she laid my baby in a nest of pillows on the bed and brought two glasses of iced tea from the kitchen. Except for Jessica, it was as if I had never been gone.

The mountain looms over us as summer blurs into autumn and autumn into a long, dark winter. At last, ice melts in the creek, and spring comes to a valley still patched with snow. As the days warm and lengthen, we pick dandelion greens and handfuls of violets, watch tadpoles in the shrinking puddles in the rutted lane. Soon, I know, the water will dry up and most of them will die.

Aunt Esta's moods come more often now. Like fog, they descend without warning, and when her mind wanders, her body is inclined to follow. Restless, confused and contrary, she prowls at night, her steps scraping along the rough wood floors. I sleep with one eye open and drag through the days exhausted.

Yesterday, just after sun up, I found her bed empty. After searching the house, and making sure Jessica was still asleep, I ran to the road. In the distance, I saw her hobbling along, headed for the wide belt of trees at the foot of the mountain. She gripped a digging fork in her fist, and a basket bumped against her hip as she walked.

I fell into step beside her, a little out of breath and anxious to get back to my child, yet knowing better than to question or argue. "You're out early this morning," I said.

"Gonna dig me some 'sang. Them city fellas, greedy pigs, they be comin' to steal my 'sang."

"It's too early for ginseng, Aunt Esta. See?" I pointed to the trees, just beginning to show green. "We'll go dig 'sang this fall, you and me and Jessie, when the leaves turn."

She stood, head back, mouth open, staring at the delicate leaves against the whitewashed sky. Then she nodded and turned back toward home. "'When the maples blaze red as my sweet Esta's hair,' my daddy always said. That's the time to dig the 'sang." She smiled and patted the cottony fuzz, so thin her scalp showed pink in the morning light, and for an instant, I caught a glimpse of something I had not seen before.

When we turned into the overgrown lane, past lush pillows of pink and white phlox, I heard Jessica screaming. Heart pounding, I ran for the house, hating this place, hating the mountain. Hating what kept me here.

Jessie stood shaking the rail of her crib, tear stained, red faced and frightened. Furious.

"Mad as an old wet hen, ain't she?" Aunt Esta chortled.

I gathered the snuffling baby to me, and feeling her soggy diaper wetting the front of my dress, I laughed. "She sure is, Aunt Esta. Just like an old wet hen." Burying my face in the soft, sweaty little neck, I suddenly thought of a little girl with hair as red as maples in autumn.

I tied a bell to the door, and twice during the night I was awakened as Aunt Esta, in nightgown and boots, with digging fork and basket, stepped out into the darkness. When finally I got her settled back into bed, I collapsed in my own bed, exhausted. I awoke, not from any sound, but perhaps from the lack of sound, something missing that should have been there. The bell, its cord neatly cut, lay on the table. Aunt Esta was gone.

From the end of the path, my eyes strained into the gray dawn, but she was nowhere in sight. I knew she was on the mountain. With the uncertain light, the loose rocks, her wavering gait . . . *Oh, my God!* Running back to the house, I scooped Jessie from her bed and wrapped her in a quilt. The little head bobbed like an orange spilled from a Christmas stocking, and stones bruised my slippered feet as, desperate, I ran toward the darker gray that was the mountain.

Aunt Esta, please don't be hurt. Oh, God, please don't let her be dead. Filmy scarves of mist floated in the trees, and birds began their first sleepy twittering. I thought of all the years Aunt Esta had cared for me, how she had accepted me—and my child—without question.

Now thoroughly awake, wet, hungry and frightened, Jessica howled. I pressed her face into my shoulder as branches stung my face and tangled in my hair. Clearing the trees, I scanned the lower slopes for some movement. I saw nothing. Nothing. I began to climb, panting, shifting my awkward, squalling bundle from arm to arm. I knew exhaustion—and Jessie—would soon force me to give up the search.

I found Aunt Esta halfway up the lower slope, sitting on a rock, looking out over the valley. Her fork and basket lay beside her.

"A bit early for 'sang," she said, looking at me as if she expected some argument.

"Maybe a little," I agreed, sinking down beside her. Her arm against mine was icy, and she shivered in the damp morning air. I drew her to me and pulled the quilt over the three of us. Snuggling into the warmth, Jessie was soon asleep.

"This old mountain, she always be here," Aunt Esta said, patting the rock we sat on.

"Just like a big old spider," I said, continuing the familiar litany.

Back from her shadowy world, Aunt Esta stroked my hand under the cover. "No," she said, the quavering old voice becoming strong. "Not a spider. I think she be like a mother hen, an old mother hen, gathering all her little biddies safe under her wing."

Below, dogwood and redbud emerged in the growing light. Jessie sighed and nestled closer.

"Maybe so, Aunt Esta. Maybe so."

Together we watched as the sun crowned the mountain, burning away the mist, chasing shadows across the valley floor.

The Waiting Room

It was hot that day—hot and hazy. Funny isn't it—the things you remember? I mean, here's this antiseptic little man with his antiseptic little voice, telling me what no one should ever have to hear, and what do I remember? The weather, for godsake.

And his shoes. I can still see those shoes, scuffed and worn, at odds with the crisp white jacket and creased trousers. He came around the huge desk in his office and perched on the polished wood in front of me, like he'd done this before.

I heard his voice, recognized the words, but they made no sense. The gray haze pressing against the window had somehow seeped into my brain, and the more I tried to concentrate, the less I understood. What was he saying? I shook my head and watched that sorry looking shoe swing back and forth in front of me. Back and forth . . . back and forth.

I don't remember stepping from the air-conditioned office into that sweltering July afternoon, but I was on the street, walking through a mirage of pavement and people and buildings, and nothing was real except the heat and the haze around me.

I must have walked for blocks, because when I approached the parking lot, it was from the wrong direction. I saw a drunk, staggering between the cars like a roach sprayed with Raid. Poor soul, I thought. Probably hasn't had a bath or a decent meal in weeks. Then I began to laugh, a laugh that started deep and dark and grew until it burst around me in jagged shards. Poor soul? He'd probably live forever, pickled liver and all, while I . . .

The haze swirled, cleared for an instant, and the doctor's words finally broke through—a few weeks, maybe a couple of months. July, August, September. Autumn, my favorite time of year. I don't know where the words came from, but I heard them. "Nooo! Oh, God, no!"

The drunk, shocked nearly sober, stared at the crazy woman two cars away, blinked, then raised a grubby paper bag to his lips. Fortified, he wiped his mouth with the back of his hand, shrugged and ambled off.

I don't remember driving home, but I was in the kitchen with my back against the door, and my husband Jack was sitting at the table. I hadn't thought about how I would tell him, what I would say. "I'm dying," I blurted. Just like that. "I'm dying."

"Yeah, me too," he said between bites of Kentucky Fried Chicken. "This heat's a real bitch."

He didn't even stop gnawing on that damned drumstick.

Finally he got it. He hit the wall with his fist—hard—so hard that one of my mother's plates, the one with the bluebirds and the twenty-four karat gold rim, fell and broke into tiny pieces. That's when I began to cry. I cried until morning crowded the darkness into the corners of the room. Then I called Jenny.

What can I say about Jenny? I remember when she was born, although Mother still insists that's not possible. *You weren't even two years old. How could you remember?* But I do. I remember a wriggling blanket making strange noises. Tiny toes that curled at my touch. A wrinkled red bottom dusted with sweet smelling powder. Then, a few months later, arms and legs and rump so smooth and round my sharp new teeth ached to taste them—a temptation, Mother tells me, I did not always resist.

How could I tell Jenny? What could I say? I don't know what I said, but Jenny came, and she held me, repeating my name over and over. Oh, Jill . . . Jill. We both cried, and I comforted her. Old habits die hard.

I haven't cried since.

I take two weeks vacation, then personal leave from my job. *Illness in the family*, I tell my boss when pressed for a reason. Somehow the thought of facing the three walls in my tiny cubicle, staring into that blank, black screen with its pulsing cursor, for one more minute—one more second even—seems obscene.

Except for Jack and Jenny, I have told no one of my illness, but the news spreads as quickly and as insidiously as the thing growing inside me. At first, I get a blizzard of cards and letters and calls. I hear from people I haven't heard from in years—some I'm not sure I ever knew. Then nothing. My friends, most of them, seem embarrassed; they don't know what to say. If we happen to meet, they look everywhere but into my eyes.

Denise, my office buddy, phones. She laughs nervously, talks too much, too fast. Then the flood carries her where she never intended to go. "You're gonna die when you hear this," she says. Silence spreads like a fungus. It oozes through the receiver, stifles me with its fetid spores. I can see Denise, her fair skin flushed red, her mouth open in dismay. I want to say, *It's all right, Denise; don't worry about it.* But the silence is too intense. She's crying as she stammers an excuse and hangs up.

The summer becomes an orgy of cruel and unusual punishment. Five days a week, Jenny, my beautiful, healthy sister Jenny, drives me to the clinic, and we sit in the waiting room filled with other victims—bald, hollow-eyed skeletons—and I promise myself I will not become one of them. I think of concentration camps as I watch them go, one by one, and I vow that I will not, I *will not* follow. But when my name is called, Jenny squeezes my hand, and I rise obediently, allow myself to be punctured and poisoned, and when finally it is over, I agree to return another day. What else can I do?

I think about one Friday evening several months ago when a gang from the office stopped at a little hole-in-the-wall bar. We got started on this silly game, *What would you do if...* After a couple of rounds, someone asked, "What would you do if you had only a year to live?"

Cathy watched our handsome waiter walk away and giggled. "Just give me a year with him, and I'll die happy."

"I'd settle for a few nights," Denise chimed in, and we all laughed.

Sue said she would have to spend the entire year on her knees, repenting of past sins; otherwise, she was bound for hell for sure. I don't remember what I said.

The strange thing is, you don't do anything exotic; you don't chuck it all and sail off to Tahiti. On good days I putter around the house, do the dishes and a little laundry. Maybe dust a room or two, cook dinner. Familiar, ordinary things. Sometimes it almost seems that dying isn't so much different from living.

One day I made strawberry jam. I stood over the boiling pot, breathing in that sweet summer smell, just like last year. Later, when the jars were labeled and lined up on the shelf, glowing like rubies, I stood for a long time looking at them, wondering—and this is the difference—wondering who would open those jars and spread that jam on hot buttered toast, or mix it in oatmeal, or maybe eat it with a spoon straight from the jar.

In the evenings I sit in the yard alone, watching the hummingbirds dart and hover at the feeder, listening as the cicadas reel in yet another day, wondering how many days I have left. That, too, is the difference.

I stay until the light is nearly gone and the air is heavy with dew and the sweet fragile smell of grass, and fireflies rise like sparks in a gust of wind. Finally, when the moon snags in the tall pine that was our Christmas tree not so many years ago, and the sky is full of stars, and Jack has asked for the third time when I'm coming in, I surrender the day.

He asks me what I want from him, this man I married a thousand years ago, when *'til death do us part* was just a romantic notion, and I tell him, "Nothing. I just want to be alone." But that's a lie. What I want—I want him to take me in his arms and love me so fiercely that I forget that gleaming desk and those Salvation Army shoes, to possess me so completely that I lose count of the days until September. Why doesn't he know that?

Why can't I tell him?

Time has missed a beat and lost its rhythm. It races as I spend my precious horde of days, then stands still as Jenny and I sit together in the waiting room. I look around me. Poor pitiful souls. Funny. You'd think such awful misery would create a bond, but it doesn't. No fraternity here. Instead, if we chance to meet on the street or at the supermarket or pharmacy, we just nod and walk on.

I study the gaunt faces, the deep, dark eyes, and know that I am looking into a mirror. Maybe that's why we deny our kinship. Just before I shudder at the horror of it, Jenny moves closer and puts her arm around me. Jenny always knows. Sometimes it's like we live in the same skin.

That's how it should be with someone you love. That's how I thought marriage would be, but it isn't. At least not mine. I never know what Jack is thinking. Now it seems that he is always angry. At the doctors, the insurance company. At me. Maybe at himself. How would I know? We don't talk much. Come to think of it, we never did.

I see him watching me, and it bothers me. Does he expect to see the Angel of Death hovering over my shoulder? Or maybe he thinks that chariot will swing down and take me up to heaven, like old Elijah.

I think about that, about whether I'll go to heaven. If there *is* a heaven. Sometimes at night I imagine St. Peter adding up my sins—big sins, little sins, middle-size sins—passing them over a scanner like a cashier at Wal-Mart, and I wonder if there's enough in my account to cover them.

And late as it is, I turn right around and smash another commandment. Like yesterday. Jenny drove up in her new convertible, her bare midriff perfect under the striped crop top, tanned legs sprouting out of white shorts, thick shining hair pulled back with a wide red band. I looked at her, and—God forgive me—as much as I love her, I envied her. Her health, her energy. Her hair. Oh, God, how I coveted all that hair.

"So, how's Jack and Jill?" she asked, just as she has asked every time she's talked to me since Jack and I started dating.

"Jack?" she said way back when it all began. "Jill, you can't! You wouldn't!"

I poked my fingers in her ribs, and we collapsed on the ruffled bedspread in my virginal bedroom, giggling like ten-year-olds.

"So, how's Jack and Jill?" she said yesterday, just like always, and somehow things didn't seem quite so bad.

I put on half the clothes in my closet to protect my poor tortured body from the sun, and we went for a ride in the new car her husband Phil gave her for their sixth anniversary. He's a dentist and spoils her rotten, but that's okay. Jenny deserves to be spoiled.

She drove fast, and the wind took my breath away. The feel of the wind blowing through my wispy hair was delicious. It was good to be cruising along, talking and laughing just like old times, and for a while I forgot to count the days until September.

Jack left on the twenty-first of August. One night, late, I found him in the den, watching the test pattern on TV. I could tell he was upset, but when I tried to put my arms around him, he pushed me away. "Get away from me," he said. "Just get out of here and leave me alone."

"What's wrong? What have I done?"

"You haven't done anything, for chrissake. Just leave me alone." His voice was cold and hard, and the look on his face was like nothing I have ever seen before, an awful mask of love and hate and grief and rage. Then he was crying, his shoulders shaking with great heaving sobs. "It's the waiting. I can't take any more of this goddamn waiting. If you're going to die, just do it. Just go ahead and do it." He looked at me with such pain that I thought I just *might* die right then and there. Then he went into the bedroom and locked the door.

I slept on the couch that night, and when I woke up the next morning, he was gone.

It's a funny thing about time. It goes on, regardless of how much you hurt, or how much you want to hang on to every minute, or how much you just want it all to end. September's come and gone, and I'm too sick to enjoy the blue and gold of October. I've lost twenty-eight pounds and my hair and eyebrows. My face has the blank, surprised look of a mannequin in a store window, and, like the mannequin, my eyes are flat and lifeless.

My fingers explore the unfamiliar territory of my naked scalp. I think that, with the thing gnawing away inside me like a rat nibbling on cheese, the baldness shouldn't matter, but it does. It matters.

Marybeth, my Hospice volunteer, helps with all the things that must be done whether you're living or whether you're dying—the shopping and the cooking and the dishes. And Jenny comes every day. It seems like a lifetime since she last asked, *So, how's Jack and Jill?* Now she says, "So. Have you heard from that miserable sonofabitch?"

I say I haven't, but I hear he's drinking too much and missing work.

Again, just like yesterday and the day before and the day before that, she begs me to come and live with her and Phil in their big house.

"Not yet," I say. "Not yet." I look around me at the familiar room, the furniture, the pictures on the wall, neat and predictable and unchanged, and know I cannot leave.

October passes, and suddenly it's Thanksgiving. I'm done with chemo, at least for a little while. Already I've gained two pounds. My hair is starting to grow back, darker and curlier than before. The summer and fall have been a litany of last times, and now, with winter approaching, I will have no more of it. No more last times.

A fat roasting chicken thaws in the sink, and a lone yam waits in the vegetable bin. I hear a key in the lock and Jenny swirls into the room on a draft of cold air. I notice that she is pale this morning, and her eyes are different, shadowed and flat, as if she's focused deep inside herself. I know, even before she tells me, that she's pregnant.

"When?" I ask.

"July." Her eyes fill with tears and she throws her arms around me. "You're getting better," she says. "You are." She swipes at the tears with her thumb and gives me a gentle shake. "You're going to make it. You hear?"

I nod, because she expects me to.

Later, she stands at the door, patting her white rabbit fur earmuffs, and I try to remember how many birthdays have passed since I gave her those silly things.

"*Please* spend Thanksgiving with us," she says for the umpteenth time as she buttons her short red coat.

"Not this year."

I hug her tight, and she goes down the sidewalk, her breath like puffs of cotton in the clear cold air. At the car, she turns and waves, and I see she's wearing the silly fur mittens that match the silly fur earmuffs. I laugh, a strange, foreign sound. I haven't laughed in a long, long time.

Maybe Jenny's right. Maybe. I try to imagine my body healing, growing strong and healthy. The coppery taste from the chemo is fading, and I'm beginning to enjoy food again. This morning I opened the first jar of strawberry jam. It tasted like summer. I find myself anticipating Thanksgiving dinner, the roast chicken, my lonely yam and the pumpkin pie Jenny brought.

But now I sit at the window watching the first tentative snowflakes as I address Christmas cards, just as I have done for years. My mind fast-forwards through Christmas, to spring. Summer. Jenny's baby. Dare I hope for another summer-ripened September?

But now. Right now. Snow filters through the trees and drifts in random patterns on the grass. I hold my breath to listen to its sound against the windows—a peculiar mix of whisper and sigh. The flow of warm air from the furnace circulates the spicy aroma of Jenny's pie and another fragrance, so subtle I can't put a name to it.

I open my address book to the "A's" and uncap my pen. But slowly. Slowly. My fingers memorize the texture of the envelopes. My eyes feast on the reds and blues and greens and golds, and I think a long time about the message I write in each card.

Permission To Leave

You flail the walls
of this earthen cocoon,
frightened, desperate, seeking,
like the redbird trapped
that day in our barn,
frantic wings beating, beating
feathered prints on dusty pane,
fragrant hay stained red.
And I took it in my hands,
frail body, battered, bleeding,
held it until it could fly;
and it soared over the meadow,
red stitching blue and green.

You struggle to shed
this crumbling shell,
to breach the invisible wall.
Yet I beg you to stay
one minute,
one heartbeat.
Don't go . . .
Don't go . . .
Don't go . . .

But I think of the redbird,
how it flew from my hand,
red streaking blue and green,
so I kiss you once
and open my hands
and let you fly.

Important Things—1941

Obsession
Concession
Oppression

Jackboots churning
London burning
Young men turning old
in the warp of war.

but I was two
knew only my mother's arms
my father's voice
and a ragged brown bear
tattered and torn
battered and worn thin
by love.

The Greatest Danger

The air conditioner broke down today, and now, near midnight, I lie awake in the stifling bedroom. Beside me, my husband sleeps soundly. Shadows from the willow tree trail across the wall, and I strain to catch the breeze that moves them. Finally, I slide out of bed, tiptoe to Lisa's room. She, too, sleeps, arms and legs outstretched like a starfish tangled in the sheets. I see the gentle rise and fall of her chest, hear the sweet whisper of her breath, and the heat coils around the dread in me, embellishing it with awful possibilities.

I slip out of the house, light a citronella candle, and sit on the patio in the humid night, watching the cool and distant moon, wondering how, finally, to tell my daughter what she now must know. The smoke from the candle spirals up and out. I breathe its pungent scent and search for a way around tomorrow.

I was fifteen and pregnant when I married the first time. Roy was thirty.

"It's better than jail," he told me with a harsh little laugh, "but not much."

There was no honeymoon. That first night, our wedding night, I fried hamburgers—one of the few things I knew how to cook—stuck a couple of candles in empty beer bottles, and waited for my new husband to come home. He did, at three a.m., dead drunk and in a rage. Chairs crashed against the wall, glass shattered, filthy names clouded the air.

And the evening and the morning were the first day of many long days to come.

Finally, after months of abuse, afraid he would one day kill me, I went back home. Mom kept my baby, a little girl named Lisa, while I worked at the Go-Mart and studied for my G.E.D. I had a year of peace. Then Roy called. I had deserted him, he said. He was divorcing me. He said I had to go to his lawyer's office and sign some papers.

Glad to be out of it, not knowing I was only giving my misery room to grow, I went, did as I was told. Too late I learned that among the papers I signed was a joint custody agreement. Lisa was to be all his every other weekend.

"She's sick," I lied that first weekend. "She can't go."

He gave a nasty laugh. "She'd better get well real quick, or your sorry ass is gonna land in jail."

Within an hour, a deputy, one of his buddies, was pounding on the door.

"He's the law," Mom said behind me. "You'd better let her go."

I was seventeen-years-old, a high school dropout. What did I know about the law? How could I stop someone like Roy? I let her go.

He was living in a trailer on the edge of town with a girl named Gloria who was, as he put it, *keeping house* for him. Lisa came home from those visits hungry and filthy, first screaming for hours, then becoming listless. By the time she was back to normal, it was time for another visit with Daddy.

When he brought her home on the evening of her second birthday, her face was pink and her eyelashes were singed. He said she had gotten too close to the candles, but instinctively my hand went to my own eyes, and I felt again the horror of his hand, like a vise on my head, forcing my face closer and closer to the burner on the gas stove in our apartment.

I watched him drive away, then, with my baby snuffling against my neck, stumbled to the kitchen. Mom was baking pies. Apple. I sucked in that delicious fragrance, knowing it was the last time I would smell pies baking in this house.

"We're leaving, Mom. Now. Tonight."

She turned from the crust she was rolling, wiped her hands on her apron, looked at me, looked at Lisa. "Wait 'til morning. I'll go with you."

Something in her face told me she was remembering the abuse she had taken from my father. "God help her," was all she said when Dad finally left with a younger woman.

"We'll need money," she said. "I'll go to the bank in the morning."
I knew she couldn't have much.

We drove east in the rain, stopping only to gulp down the coffee and sandwiches and apple pie we had brought. Around seven o'clock that evening, we crossed the Ohio River into West Virginia. Behind us, a violent sunset bled through purple clouds, its colors reflecting on the wet pavement ahead. If it was an omen, I didn't know what to make of it—good, or bad.

Half an hour later, hungry and tired, we stopped at a diner to eat. It was clean, and the waitress—the name embroidered on her pocket was Connie—was friendly.

"This looks like a good place," Mom said. "Why don't we stop here?"

"Do you think it's far enough?"

She nodded.

"Any apartments for rent around here?" I asked Connie as she refilled our glasses of iced tea.

She pointed overhead. "Old man that lived up there died a few weeks ago. Wasn't much of a housekeeper, I'm afraid. It's pretty grubby." She smiled at Lisa and yelled over her shoulder. "Hey, Bernie, these folks are askin' about the apartment."

Bernie was short and thin, bow-legged and fussy neat, in a crisp white apron and a chef's hat almost as tall as he was. He looked at Lisa. She shrank into a corner of the booth and popped her thumb in her mouth. My heart sank.

"She's real good," I began, but he shook his head.

"Oh, kids are no problem. I've got one about her age that I don't get to see much of. Lives in Bluefield with her mother."

Connie wasn't exaggerating. The apartment was filthy. But it's amazing what a week's worth of soap, hot water and elbow grease can do. Bernie even sprung for a couple gallons of paint. It wasn't *House Beautiful*, but it was home.

I worked seven to three at the diner while Mom kept Lisa. Then she worked a few hours at night at the bakery down the street. Not the best way to live with a rambunctious two-year-old, but between the two of us, we managed to make ends meet.

For several months, Lisa woke at night, screaming, her eyes, wild with fright, straining into the darkness. "Daddy," she would say, pointing. "Daddy."

She wanted nothing to do with any man. Bernie adored her, but bless his heart, he played it cool. When Mom brought her downstairs for her breakfast, there was usually some small toy on the highchair tray, but he pretended to ignore her.

At last, her curiosity—and the ridiculous hat—became too much for her. "Hat?" she said one morning, as Bernie, eyes straight ahead, walked past her. Still not looking at her, he took off the hat and carefully placed it on her head.

She giggled and patted his face. "Thanks, Bernie," she said, gracious as a queen bestowing a knighthood, and from that moment on, Bernie was her slave. As she grew accustomed to him, learned to trust him, the nightmares became less frequent and finally stopped.

In those first months, when I jumped at every phone call, held my breath every time the door opened, searched every face for signs of recognition, I noticed Bernie watching me. Then, like he was reading my mind, he would touch my shoulder in the gentlest way. It was a new thing to me, that gentleness, and I drank it in, hoarded it for the next dry season.

People talk about falling in love, but there was no falling to it. It was more like a stroll through autumn woods, with the sky so blue and clear through the brilliant trees, and the leaves floating down around us like blessings.

I told him all the things I thought I could never tell anyone; about what had happened to me, what I knew had happened to Lisa, and he cried.

Years passed, and that other life seemed more and more like a bad dream. With Bernie, we were cherished. We were safe. Then, there he was. Roy. Standing at the plate glass door of the diner, beckoning to me. He had changed in five years—older, thinner, seedier—but the way he gripped my arm, digging his fingers in until I winced, was the same.

"You whorin' slut," he breathed into my face. "Where's my kid?"

I shook my head, and the pressure on my arm increased. "How did you find me?" I whispered through stiff lips, praying Lisa wouldn't pick that moment to come downstairs from Mom's apartment.

"Your old man died a couple'a months ago, right? Worthless ol' bastard, probably the only decent thing he ever done." He laughed and spit just inches from my foot. "And his only daughter, a Mrs. Rebecca Brown, of Ashford, West Virginia, was in for the funeral, right?"

I had been careful, worn a scarf and glasses, spoken to no one. "Nobody knew that! How did you find me?"

"Oh, you made quite a splash. Why, accordin' to this newspaper piece my friend sent me, that funeral must'a been the social event of the season. Honey, I always told you, you can't get away from an ol' hound dog like me. Not permanent, anyways."

How had the newspaper gotten my name, my location? Then, I remembered. I had written a check for gas on the way out of town. How could I have forgotten there were no secrets in that place?

"Where is she?" He was shaking me like a pup shakes an old sock when Bernie came charging through the door, bandy legs pumping, hat billowing like a sail in a storm. I had never seen anything so beautiful. Roy backed away, spewing filth with every step. "Tomorrow, bitch. Have her here tomorrow, or you're gonna be real sorry."

And now, tomorrow is only hours away. How can I tell Lisa that not all men are like the strong and gentle man she calls Poppy? That, but for a foolish, headstrong young girl, none of this would have happened? But then, of course, there would be no Lisa. So where's the sense of it? How do you explain it all to a seven-year-old?

I hear the screen door open, close, and Bernie is behind me, kneading my neck and shoulders, resting his cheek against my hair, as if to protect me from all the grief that Roy carries in his mean little heart.

"We've got to leave, Bernie," I say. "I can't see any other way."

He's in front of me now, squatting on the bricks, lacing his fingers in mine. "Running's not the answer, sweetheart. You know I'd go in a minute if I thought it was." He looks at the big comfortable house, the clipped lawn and the neat flowerbeds. "None of this is worth a damn without you and Lisa."

I pull his hand, still linked with mine, to my face, swipe at the tears running down my cheeks. "I don't know what to do; I just don't know what to do."

"It's going to be all right, Becky. Trust me. Please." He puts his arm around me and guides me back to bed.

The room cools, and the shadows on the wall grow still in that peculiar hush before dawn. Finally, I sleep.

When I awake, Bernie is at the mirror, ready for work. In his hand, he holds a thick envelope.

He comes to sit on the bed, takes a paper from the envelope. "I went to see my lawyer this morning. This . . . " he shakes the paper and it rattles like dry leaves. "This says that one Roy Groves, being the natural father of a minor, Lisa Groves, waives all parental rights, including visitation." He folds the paper into the envelope and slaps it against his hand. "Me and ol' Roy have a little business to take care of."

"He'll never sign that, Bernie. You know he won't."

"He'll sign it. One way or another, he'll sign." Bernie's mouth is a grim line. "Take Lisa to Mom's and tell her to make sure she stays there."

It's three o'clock before Roy shows up, between the lunch and dinner crowds, when the diner is almost empty. He swaggers through the door, thumbs hooked in his belt loops. "I don't see no kid," he says, looking around.

"Have a seat," Bernie says, polite as can be. "Sweetheart, bring the man a cup of coffee."

My nerves are shot. Coffee sloshes into the saucer as I set it down. Bernie takes the paper from his pocket, smoothes it out, and slides it across the table. Then, slowly, one by one, he deals out ten one hundred dollar bills. He smiles, a smile I have never seen before, hands Roy a pen and says just one word. "Sign."

Roy looks at the pen, the money, the agreement.

Oh, Bernie. I think of all the long hot hours that are spread out on that table, but Roy's going to sign it! I can't believe it! He's going to sign!

At that moment, Lisa comes tearing down the stairs, laughing, hair flying, Mom at her heels. "Poppy!" she cries, holding out her arms. Then she sees Roy, stops, her eyes wide and vacant, as if every nightmare she has ever had is playing in her head. "You . . . " she says, her lips barely moving. "You . . . "

I see him coil, lunge toward her, but I'm frozen, unable to move.

Like a tiger hungry for blood, Bernie springs, and Mom hustles Lisa upstairs. I've seen it on TV, a big cat bringing down much larger prey, and I have to remind myself that these are not animals. Bernie is on him, dragging him through the kitchen door to the grill, forcing his head down. I hear Bernie growl, "Remember this? Goddamn you, she was just a baby." The head goes down a degree at a time, lower, and lower, and lower.

Something dark and savage in me welcomes the screams, feeds on the terror. I want to see him suffer. I want to see him die. But lose gentle Bernie? Oh, no. I grip his shoulder. "Don't, Bernie. Let him go."

Through my fingertips I can feel the struggle as he forces the wild thing back into its hiding place. Then he relaxes, shoves Roy, cowed and quivering, through the door to the table. Deliberately, Bernie gathers up the money, folds it and puts it back into his pocket. He hands Roy the pen and says very, very quietly, "Sign it."

Roy signs and sidles out the door, a cruel little man, and dangerous. But I see now the greatest danger is not Roy himself; it's the violence he spreads like a deadly virus. Shivers crawl up my arms and prickle my scalp as I realize even my Bernie is not immune. Nor am I.

We stand side by side, Bernie and I, not touching, not looking at each other, two strangers suddenly stripped naked. Roy peels away from the curb, black smoke puffing from the exhaust. The smell of oil and burning rubber settles around us.

We watch until he turns onto Route 50, headed out of town.

Crossword

"Lazy bum, get a job!" Avis, perched on the couch in the living room, was in a snit as usual.

Harry winced. That voice! Might as well have your ears scrubbed with steel wool. The trailer baked in a late September heat wave, and he eased his sweaty back away from the plastic chair.

"Get a job," she repeated, but Harry didn't answer, just turned down his hearing aid and went on working his crossword puzzle. He had learned that was the only way to handle her tirades. That, or wring her scrawny little neck.

She sounded just like his boss at the mill. Always giving orders. Do this. Do that. He had finally taken care of that problem by getting himself fired, but now he had Avis to contend with.

He couldn't figure out how to get rid of her, couldn't remember what had possessed him to take up with her in the first place. Loneliness? Sure he was lonely after Helen died, but it was something more. Maybe a hunger for the exotic. Maybe knowing he didn't have that much longer to do something wild and crazy.

And Avis was different then, gorgeous, dressed in shimmering blues and greens and golds. "Hello, there," she had said in a sultry voice as he prowled the aisles of his favorite pet store, looking for something special for his cat, Mitzi. Avis blinked slowly, moved toward him with seductive little steps. She was flashy. Exciting. Maybe that was why, when he left the store, Avis went, too.

Right from the start there was trouble. Avis hated Mitzi, and Mitzi was scared to death of her. Mitzi, poor little thing, tried to be friendly. But whenever she came within range of those beady eyes, Avis began screeching at her in language so vile the air turned blue.

Within a month Mitzi was dead. Harry found the pathetic lump of black and white fur huddled behind the couch. There wasn't a mark on the body, but he knew Avis had something to do with it. He should have ended it right then.

Sweat glued him to the plastic chair, and he shifted uncomfortably. God, he hated this heat. Avis, on the other hand, thrived on it. The hotter the better. Well, he had news for old Foul Mouth. He'd had enough of this weather; he was heading north, to a fishing camp he remembered. Cool breezes, lazy waves slapping against the shore. Peace and quiet. Maybe if she had to fend for herself for a while, she'd be a little easier to get along with.

He threw a few necessities into the homemade camper and hitched it to his rattletrap truck. But before he could make his getaway, Avis, furious, came flying out of the trailer, making such a racket that he finally opened the door and let her in. Goodbye, peace and quiet. Yet, with his hearing aid turned down and the old truck headed north, he was almost happy.

By the time they crossed the Pennsylvania border into New York, black clouds were boiling up in the northeast. The radio crackled with static, and Harry turned up his hearing aid just in time to catch a weather advisory. "Hear that, Avis?" he said with a nasty grin. "It's gonna get colllld. Might even snow. You'd like that, wouldn't you?"

Avis, shivering in the passenger seat, made a rude noise and huddled deeper into her tropical colors.

Let it snow, Harry thought, watching her discomfort with pleasure. *Don't make no never mind to me.* It wasn't far now, and the camper had a good heater.

He turned onto a dirt road, rutted and overgrown. As the old truck rattled deep into the tunnel of trees, he searched for familiar landmarks, but found none. Darkness fell like a curtain. Then the engine sputtered and died. Sleet stung Harry's face as he climbed out of the truck and dashed for the camper. Silent for once, Avis clung to his arm. They were hardly in the door, though, when she started in again. "Stupid. Damned stupid man."

He lit a lantern and went to work on the stove. It smoked a little, but it would keep them warm. Might as well make the best of it. Avis glared at him as he took out his crossword puzzle and lit a cigarette. Seven down . . . Iranian coins. Five letters. He thought for a minute, shook his head, then went on. Twenty-two across . . . Rare bird. Eight letters. His mouth twisted in a wry smile as he penciled in the letters . . . R A R A . . .

But there was to be no peace that night. Avis' complaints went on and on and on. She was cold. She was hungry. Poor Avis. Always poor Avis. Her voice, that voice that had once fascinated him, rubbed his nerves like sandpaper.

Finally, he couldn't take any more. "Shut up!" he yelled, grabbing her. "You think you're cold now, do you? Well, see how you like this!" He opened the door and threw her out into the freezing darkness.

For a while, even with his hearing aid turned off, he could hear her hoarse cries, hear her thumping against the camper, trying to get into the truck. Then he heard nothing.

John Duffy was a big beefy man, built low to the ground like a basset hound. In more than thirty years as coroner, he figured he had seen it all. He wedged his bulk through the narrow door of the camper and stood with hands on his hips. Harry still sat in the chair, the crossword puzzle in front of him. Duffy picked it up, slapped it against his hand, and stuffed it into his jacket pocket. "He's dead all right," he said to his assistant, a first-year intern named Kelly. "Dead as a mackerel." He bent over the stove, hands on his knees. It had long since run out of fuel. "Gotta be carbon monoxide," he said, looking at the flue running through the ceiling.

Outside he hoisted himself up the ladder at the rear of the camper. Reaching the top, he realized he hadn't seen anything until now.

"Hey, Kelly, get up here. Bring the camera."

His short legs hit the ground, and he stood chomping on an unlit cigar as Kelly scampered up the ladder. Kelly stared at the bizarre scene on top of the camper, looked down at his boss in disbelief. Avis sprawled atop the flue, her bright colors shimmering through a crust of ice. "A parrot?" he said. "A parrot offed the old geezer?"

"Appears that way. Must've roosted on the flue, trying to keep warm."

"A parrot?" Kelly repeated. "Where'd it come from?"

"Damned if I know," the coroner answered. "Probably somebody's pet."

Headed back to town with Kelly driving, Duffy pulled the crossword puzzle from his pocket. "I must be addicted to these things," he said, grinning sheepishly. "Can't stand to see one unfinished."

Seven down, Iranian coins. R I A L S. Twenty-two across, Rare bird.

R A R A... That was as far as the poor old codger had gotten. Slowly, as if he were carving stone, Duffy completed the block...

A V I S.

The Taste Of Vengeance

Two things I remember of that day in the meadow—the taste of wild strawberries, summer-warm and sweet, and the baby rabbit, huddled like a lawn ornament in the tall grass. My father, half a step ahead of our dog Bounce, scooped it up and held it against his chest.

The rabbit's eyes were squeezed shut, ears flat against its back. "It's scared to death," my father said, stroking the soft fur. I traced one silky ear with a tentative finger and felt the fear travel up my arm.

Now, years later, in the emergency room at the hospital, I hold my daughter tight against me. Tiny, so young, she perches on the edge of the examination table like a bird about to fly. She's sobbing and hysterical, her clothes muddy and torn. Her face is bruised, knees skinned, the palms of both hands bloody, with bits of gravel ground into the flesh. I touch her cheek and her anguish vibrates through me.

"There were two of them, Mom. They wanted money, and all I had was a dollar left over from lunch. And one said . . . he grabbed me and said . . ." She crosses her arms over the tender new breasts, chokes and gags, sick with pain and humiliation. The words finally come out in a tortured croak. "He said they'd take it out in trade. Oh, Mommy!"

"It's okay, Mandy. I'm here, honey." Nausea and fury sweep through the numbness in me as I stroke the soft, sun-bronzed hair.

I pat her hand and she winces. The curtain around her bed is printed with rainbows, the walls a warm pink. I bite my lip and hold my breath against the hospital smell.

"And I ran and I ran and I ran. And they knocked me down, and I got up and ran again, and then I fell, and one kept kicking me. 'Get up, bitch. Get up and run, bitch.' He said it over and over. 'Run, bitch. Why don't you run?'"

I remember how the dog circled us, yapping and jumping, frenzied by the smell of prey. Then, with a violent shudder, the rabbit broke free. Bounce leaped and caught it midair, shook it, dropped it. Bloodied, dragging one leg, the poor creature tried to scuttle away, but it was all over. My father stared at the ground; I covered my eyes, but I heard the pitiful bleats of the rabbit long after they stopped.

Mandy's fourteen. She's in no shape to answer questions or even respond to the counselors who are on hand. She won't tell me the names of those animals, although I think she knows. She's afraid. So am I.

When it's over, when she is clean and bandaged and sedated, we go home. I lock all the doors and windows and check them again and again. I make her warm milk with honey and give her another one of the pills the emergency room doctor prescribed. Then I watch her sleep, my defenseless child, so small there is hardly evidence of a body under the blankets. She cries out in her sleep, and as I reach out, as my fingers touch the smooth forehead, I enter her nightmare.

I see her attackers as clearly as if they were standing before me—one tall and gangly, protruding ears and teeth. He's wearing a denim jacket and torn jeans. The other, pudgy and pimply, mutters, "Run, bitch, run," although he's pinning her down, his sweaty hands pawing at her clothes. The hands are grimy, grease encrusted. And I see his shirt—heavy and dark blue, with a name above the pocket. "Mitch."

Finally I tiptoe from my daughter's room, leaving the door ajar so that the glow from the hall light shines in. The nightmare vision splashes like acid, burning images into my mind. Greasy hands, dirty nails . . . blue uniform. A gas station, I think. A gas station, or maybe a garage. Mitch. I know how to find that bastard, and once I find *him*, I'll find the other one. And when I do . . . I'd like to get a gun and hunt them down like the animals they are. "Run," I'd say. "Why don't you run?" But somehow I don't think it will happen that way.

I pull the phone book from the cabinet, open it to the yellow pages. Tethered by the telephone cord, I pace, dialing one number after another. Seven times I say, "Sorry, I must have the wrong number."

But on the eighth, "Mitch? He ain't here. Left around six, I think." *Is that the voice of the other one?* Slowly I return the phone to its cradle and write down the name and address of the garage. Twenty-fourth and Maple. I know that neighborhood—it's over by the Tech College. There's a little hamburger joint—Wimpy's—on the corner where all the kids hang out. I wonder if ol' Mitch and his buddy ever eat there?

Scenes from the meadow tumble through my mind—the dog crouched over the helpless rabbit, tormenting it, nudging it to flight. I see the green grass, the sunshine and the blood in vivid color.

My father told me I shouldn't blame Bounce; it was his nature to hunt and kill. But never again did I touch that dog, or speak to him, or even look at him, and only once did I feed him scraps from the supper table.

That same evening my father found old Bounce dead. Poisoned, he said. Faintly, ever so faintly, I smelled strawberries, their fragrance released by the warmth of summer sun.

As I think of what I must do—how and when and where—I remember that Wimpy can't seem to hold on to his cooks. Could be he's looking for one right now. And suddenly, as I think about what a good cook I am, the air grows ripe with the scent of strawberries, and the taste of them is sweet, oh, so sweet.

Always The Mountain

"Hunh!" Agnes snorted, rocking and slapping her fleshy knee. "That was some highfalutin preacher! Tippy-toed all around Robin Hood's barn, he did, and when he finally got to where he was goin', damned if I could figure out where it was. I purely couldn't."

Her mouth laughed, but her eyes were crying. Agnes was like that, even when she'd just buried her only sister. "Course, I reckon it don't make no never mind to Esta. She's out of it now, God rest her soul."

"Yes," I said softly, turning the little black hat I wore to the funeral in my hands, not quite sure what to do with it. "She's out of it now."

I stood at the kitchen window, staring across the brown fields to the mountain. I could still hear Aunt Esta, plain as day. *That old mountain, she always be there.* I must have heard her say that a thousand times. I couldn't believe I'd never hear it again.

The last couple of years had been hard. Real hard. Aunt Esta's mind wandered—her body, too—and what with trying to keep up with her and my little Jessie, I was worn out. Now, I felt giddy with relief that the struggle—Aunt Esta's and mine—was over. Part of me felt so light I could fly right over that mountain, free as a bird at last. Yet, at the same time, there was this weight on me, hurting so bad I could hardly breathe.

Jessie clung to my skirt and whined. Bless her heart; she knew something was going on. I scooped her into my arms, buried my face in her sweetness and whispered nonsense in her ear.

"So, what you gonna do now, Emmy?" Agnes asked.

I settled Jessie in her highchair and gave her a cookie. The table was piled high with food: ham, potato salad, homemade bread, blackberry pie . . . Folks around here weren't much for talk at times like this. They brought what comfort they had to give in an iron pot, or wrapped in a clean dishtowel, or sealed in a Mason jar.

What was I going to do? I had no idea. Time was, I thought if I ever got away from the mountain, from this cabin where I grew up, I would never come back. But I did. I was gone just long enough to get my precious Jessie and learn that love doesn't always mean the same thing to a man as it does to a woman.

"Reckon you'll be sellin' this place," Agnes said, her hands folded over her stomach.

November wind rattled the windows, and a draft fingered my arms. "I might," I answered, looking at the rough wood floor, the bare corner where the rich earthy smell of Aunt Esta's ginseng still lingered. "Hunters were always pestering Aunt Esta to sell, but she'd chase them off every time." I smiled, remembering her in her print housedress and ragged sweater and droopy hose, shooing the men away with a twelve-gauge shotgun so rusty she couldn't have hit a post at ten paces. "Maybe I'll sell out and move to town, where Jessie can have all the things I never had."

Aunt Esta's face, hurt and shocked, floated before me. *Things? What things?* How could I have said that? No one could have loved me, cared for me, like Aunt Esta. Guilt rose and poured out in a flood of tears.

Agnes held out her arms, and I burrowed into the soft pillow of her body.

"Oh, Agnes," I sobbed. "I'm so tired. The way she couldn't seem to settle down at night . . . And she was so contrary. Sometimes I thought . . . oh, God! Sometimes I thought we would all be better off if she was gone. And now she is, and I don't know how I can stand it."

"There now," she said, patting my back. "It's all right, young'un. You just cry 'til you're done."

Drained, suddenly too tired to stand, I sank onto the straight wooden chair, and Agnes took my hand.

"You listen to me," she said. "Listen good. I had my doubts when Esta took you in after your ma and pa got theirselves killed in that accident. You, not even a blood relation, and her a widow with no babies of her own. *It'll never work*, I says to myself. Couldn't even imagine what Esta was thinkin'. Well, I was wrong. You was the best thing ever happened to her. You was Esta's blessing. She said so herself. And what would'a become of her these last few years without you? Just answer me that."

I shook my head and went back to the window. The sun rested on the rim of the mountains to the west, and shadows gathered like puddles in the yard.

I didn't sleep much that night. Agnes, who had insisted on staying over, was restless, too. It was as if Aunt Esta's spirit still prowled the creaky wooden floor. Only Jessie slept, dark lashes sweeping her cheeks, her arms thrown above her head like angel wings. She was so beautiful I felt my throat clog with tears.

I suppose it was a sin, how I got Jessie, but I loved Jeremy Campbell. Loved him, it turns out, more than he loved me. Watching her sleep, I had to believe any sin had long since been forgiven.

"Why don't you come and stay with me for a spell?" Agnes said the next morning as we sat at the scarred wooden table, drinking coffee and picking at the pound cake Dessie Sims had left.

"Oh, Agnes, I don't know. It's hunting season. Might not be safe to leave the place empty."

"All the more reason for you to get out a' here for a few days. There's always a few ain't huntin' for nothin' but trouble."

As if summoned by our words, I saw blaze orange flashing through the underbrush. The hunter picking his way toward us walked like his feet hurt. *City slicker*, I thought. *Why is it they're always wearing brand new boots?*

We watched the boots clomp up our lane to the steps. The screen door slammed behind Agnes as, arms folded, she dared the blaze-orange, camouflage-clad dandy to take one more step. Protected by her bulk, I, with Jessie in tow, followed. I swear I could hear Aunt Esta huffing at my elbow as the hunter swung his gun to the ground, the butt propped on his boot toe.

He looked me up and down, his eyes finally coming to rest a few inches below the top button of my blouse. "Your man at home?" Then, seeing Jessie clinging to my skirt, he scratched the stubble on his chin and went on, "Come to think of it, seems like I heard you ain't got a man. Just as well. Me and my buddies, we been lookin' for a piece...."

His laugh was nasty, and his gaze moved lower. "A piece of land, that is. We spotted this old shack from up on the mountain, and thought you might be interested in sellin'."

He grinned and jerked a thumb toward the cabin where I had spent most of my twenty-two years, where Aunt Esta's starched curtains hung at the windows; her herbs and dried flowers and hand-woven baskets dangled from the rafters. The old willow rocker moved gently with the draft from the open door as if she still sat there, rocking away the autumn afternoon.

Shocked, feeling dirty and exposed, I crossed my arms over my breast. Jessie whimpered and wrapped herself around my legs.

"I reckon you'd best be movin' on while you still got all your parts," Agnes said, leveling the ancient shotgun. "My aim ain't too good—tends to be a mite low. Awful, what could happen to a man."

Protecting his crotch with one hand, the man backed away, then turned and sprinted across the yard to the road.

"And don't come back!" Agnes yelled.

"That settles it," she said, turning to me. "You're comin' with me, young'un. And you ain't comin' back here 'til this craziness is over."

The sounds of killing echoed from the mountain, and as we piled into Agnes' battered Chevette, I imagined I could smell the thick warm scent of blood.

Agnes lived in a narrow little house on a narrow little street. Mondays we washed, Tuesdays we ironed, Wednesdays we sewed, just like in the song I sang when I was a kid. Every week was the same as the one before. Growing up in the isolated valley, I dreamed of life in the city. The shops, the crowds, the excitement. Exotic sights and sounds and smells. But now, in the mornings when I opened the curtains, I saw only other houses. Cars rumbled along the unpaved street in a haze of dust and exhaust. Some days the sun never quite made it through the smoke and grit from the factories along the river. The acrid smell of it was always in my nose, and the taste, like metal, in my mouth.

"What's that song you been hummin'?" Agnes asked one Monday as we hung clothes on the line.

"What? Was I humming? I didn't realize I was."

"You losin' your marbles, gal? You been hummin' it for days now, same song." She pinned a sheet to the line, blew on her cold fingers, then pinned me with a look. "Sounded to me like that old hymn we used to sing. Sounded to me a lot like *How Beautiful Upon the Mountain*."

We worked in silence for a few minutes, then she laughed. "Reckon city life ain't all it's cracked up to be. Well, young'un, give it another week. By then, all the crazies should be off your mountain, and you can go home."

Home. It wouldn't be long now.

That Friday morning, early, Sheriff Tommy Thompson came knocking at the door. I had known him ever since I could remember, and he wasn't in the habit of making social calls. Still, with Jessie safe in bed asleep, and Agnes standing beside me, how bad could it be?

"Emmy," he said, "I hate to have to tell you this." He held his hat in both hands, fingering the brim as if what he had to say was written there in Braille.

What? I wanted to shout. *What? Just say it, for God's sake! Get it over with!*

Finally, he cleared his throat and went on. "Your place burned down last night. I figure somebody broke in, probably drunk. Maybe dropped a cigarette. Maybe knocked over a lantern. Anyway, it's gone, burnt clean to the ground."

Not until we rounded the last bend in the road did I really understand what had happened. The place where the cabin had stood was black and barren. Only the chimney and the stone steps remained. Wisps of smoke still rose from the rubble, disappearing into the perfect blue sky.

"Probably some of that poor white trash that trucks in here every year," Agnes said, nudging a whiskey bottle with the toe of her shoe. "To them, huntin' ain't nothin' but one long drunken brawl."

I made my way through the destruction, stepping around the hot spots, looking for some trace of Aunt Esta, some part of her I could hold on to. I found a few coins and the charred corner of a playing card. A fork. A doorknob. But no herbs, no baskets. No willow rocker. It was all gone. Everything was gone.

I don't know how long I stood there, numb and empty. Agnes squeezed my shoulder. "Ready to go, Emmy?"

The winter day was nearly over. Shadow spilled from the mountain, sluiced down the lane, and gathered in pools around me. Shivering, I watched as the sun slid below the horizon, and the mountain vanished in darkness. Agnes shepherded me into the car, and we drove off.

I watched the place where the cabin should have been until it was out of sight. "They burned it, Agnes," I said. "The cabin, all her things..."

Agnes reached across the seat and patted my knee. "I know it hurts, honey. Hurts me, too—but houses can be rebuilt. And as far as Esta's things—that's all they was. Just things." She swerved, narrowly missing a steep drop off where the road had given way, then chuckled. "I figure ol' Esta'd be mad as hell if we needed a handful of weeds and a few sticks of wood to remember her by."

I thought about what Agnes had said as the car bored its way into the darkness, and some part of me understood, even as I grieved for what was lost. I *did* understand—finally—that this valley, the mountain, was home. In the spring, when the hills were patterned with redbud and dogwood and new green leaves, I'd be back. I'd be back with Jessie, maybe Agnes, too, to start over.

That old mountain, she always be there, Aunt Esta told me time and again. Now I knew she was right. Come morning, the mountain would rise out of the mist, just like always. Just like Aunt Esta said.

Offerings

Take some peaches, Mom urged
as she lingered between two worlds.
The percussion of her heart faltered;
her fingers groped at empty walls,
but I saw what she saw—
shelves in the musty basement
of the house where I grew up;
shelves of home-canned peaches,
golden halves overlapped
like shingles on a roof;
jars of jade beans,
blackberries plucked warm and sweet
in brambly thickets;
summer sealed in Mason jars
for the cold mountain winter.

She'd fuss with those jars
like a queen choosing jewels,
like Sunday dinner was a royal feast,
and we the guests.
She'd cook for hours,
heap her treasures on a table so full
there was hardly room for plates.
Then, aproned and flushed,
"Come eat," she'd say.
And we did—
thought little of it 'til now.

Now I see what it was she served,
what she stirred in a battered pot
with a wooden spoon.

Second Chances

It's a strange business, this sifting through the bits and pieces of a person's life after they're gone, but sooner or later, someone has to do it. Mother's been gone nearly two years, and Dad, tired of living alone, finally moved into an apartment building full of *casserole widows,* as he calls them. He grumbles, but I think he really enjoys the attention. Now, this house where I grew up, where my six-year-old daughter Meg and I have lived for the last month, is to be sold.

For days I've emptied drawers and closets. Boxes, sealed and labeled, line the walls, and the driveway is full of bulging trash bags. The musty smell of things stored and forgotten is everywhere—on my clothes, in my hair, even on my skin.

I find the button box shoved into a corner on the top shelf of the bedroom closet. Standing on tiptoe on a rickety old stool, I fish it out, wipe away the dust with my shirtsleeve, realize it hasn't been touched since Mother put it there.

Meg is sprawled on the floor with her coloring book and crayons. She's sullen and whiny. She misses her daddy; she wants to go home. Sometimes I do, too, but there comes a time you know a marriage is over, even if you don't know when or how it happened. We were happy, in love. Then one day I realized we had been neither for a long time, and what had started as fireworks blooming into beautiful patterns fizzled out with a sad little pop. I wasn't surprised when my best friend told me that Hal was having an affair. I didn't even wait for him to come home from work, just gathered up our clothes and left.

Oh, he calls, like six times a day, says he loves us, misses us. Admits to an affair, but swears it was over months ago. And, of course, it didn't mean anything. Does it ever?

I climb down with the box in my hand. "Look, Meg." I squat beside her and open the lid. "When I was a little girl, I loved to play with these."

She gives me a look that I hadn't expected to see for at least another six or seven years. Then she grabs the box and dumps it upside down on the floor. For just an instant, I'm tempted to shake her. But she's already engrossed in sorting the bits of glass and plastic and wood and metal, and my eyes begin to pick out remembered shapes.

Those little straw hats! My fingers swoop down like a jackdaw. "These were on a dress your Grammy—my mother—made me. Oh, it was awful! She couldn't sew a lick. But I loved the buttons."

Meg looks at me, almost smiles. Then I see them, all strung together on a cord, a dozen or more clear glass buttons with tiny flowers embedded in them. I reach out, touch them, hold them in my hand, see Mother as she looked that summer night when I was ten.

She may have had other dresses—probably did—but I only remember this one. It was cotton, soft from many washings, its bright flowers faded to pale pinks and purples and yellows and greens, like water colors left in the rain. She stood at the mirror in her bedroom, cheeks flushed, fingers shaking, as she fastened the buttons—these buttons—that went from neck to hem.

My mother was pretty. Everyone said so. But that night, glowing like she was, I thought she surely must be the most beautiful woman in the world. I watched as she dabbed on magic from first one jar and then another. Her hair, black with strands of early white that reminded me of shooting stars in the night sky, cracked and popped as she brushed it.

I want to tell Meg about that night, about how beautiful her grandmother was, but what do I tell her about that other figure? I can't tell her about him. I've never told anyone. Looking back, I still don't know if there was anything to tell.

She called him T.J. I remember the phone rang, and when she answered, she got that same look, all pink and glowy. He was an old friend, she said, just passing through town.

The man who stood in the light that seeped from our front room was taller than my father, but not nearly as handsome. He caught his breath as my mother stepped onto the porch. The rickety screen slapped shut, and he took her hand. They stood for a minute in the spill of light; then I heard the lazy creaking of the porch swing.

I was suddenly angry. So angry. What was he doing there with her? That was my place. Sometimes during summer vacation, she would let me sit with her, the swing just barely moving back and forth, until it was long past my bedtime. I would huddle against the warmth of her in the cool night as we watched for shooting stars and shared thick bacon sandwiches, heavy with mayonnaise, dripping juice from tomatoes picked that day from our garden. Then, when we both were too sleepy to hold our eyes open any longer, she would half guide, half carry me to bed.

I pressed my nose to the screen, smelled the sharp metal smell. I saw a long shiny car parked in the weeds beside the rutted drive that led to our house, and turning my face, I could see the two of them swaying in the old swing, his arm resting along the rough wooden back.

"Remember when we used to sit on your front porch like this?" he said.

"Ummmm. And remember how my dad always turned on the light 'long about midnight!"

They both laughed, and for a long time there was no sound except the creak of the swing and the chirp of crickets in the tall grass. Then she said, so soft I could hardly hear, "That seems like a million years ago."

I saw his hand squeeze her shoulder, heard his voice, warm and low, "Come with me."

I crept away from the door, crawled into bed and hid under the covers. I can still feel the steamy darkness, thick with sweat and tears. My head began to ache, and when I was finally forced from my cave, I could hear that old swing. Creak . . . creak . . . creak. Sometimes I still do.

I remember an old photograph album, still hidden away in the bottom bureau drawer, and with Meg absorbed in the buttons, go to find it. Sitting cross-legged on the floor, afternoon sun slanting over my shoulder, I turn the pages. I've seen the pictures before, dozens of times, but never thought much about them. Now, knowing all about broken promises, about choices, I look at them with new understanding.

They were friends, the three of them. I see them, young and untouched, arms linked, heads back, laughing. My mother, smiling at the camera. At my father. At T.J. My father, a hat pulled low over his eyes, his arm around her shoulders. T.J., his foot propped on the running board of an old car, my mother radiant, tucked into the curve of his arm. He loved her. The pictures were old and faded, but that remained clear. Did she love him? I think she loved them both, but, of course, she couldn't have both. She had to choose.

Dad worked hard, but we never had much. T.J., from the looks of his car and his clothes, was quite successful. There must have been times when she wondered what her life would have been like with him. But, given a second chance, she chose to stay, and not reluctantly, for she changed after that night. When Dad came home from work, she met him at the door with a smile and a kiss; when he spoke, she dropped everything and listened. And she couldn't seem to get enough of touching either of us. If she had any regrets, no one would ever know.

Meg, bored with the buttons, scoots over, and, perhaps sensing that I am far away, climbs into my lap. Putting her arms around my neck, she says, "I want to go home."

I bury my face in her little girl softness, see her running to meet her daddy when he comes home from work, hear her squeal as he swings her high in the air. I remember the good times, those days of cotton candy and calliopes and carousels, when fireworks lit an innocent sky, then faded to a gentle glow. Without thinking, I whisper into her hair, "I do too, baby. I do too."

I rub the buttons between my fingers, slide them one by one along the cord. Then I remember how I awoke that night to find my mother bending over me. A breeze stirred the curtains as she brushed the damp hair from my face. And, as night tiptoed toward morning, I dreamed she stood there in her pale dress, watching while I slept.

Once on a Carousel

It was September, Labor Day, and music filled the narrow valley and washed up the mountain, racing, tumbling over the rocks in rills and rivulets.

Nellie, scattering the last of the cornbread to the chickens, felt the music before she heard it. Her rhythmic, "Here, chick, here, chick chick chick," wove over and around and through it, until finally the thread of sound caught her attention. She raised her head, straining to capture the melody.

Her eyes widened and one hand tangled in her wiry gray hair as she listened. Then she turned toward the rough cottage perched halfway up the mountain. "Dan! Dan, come and listen! I can hear the carnival!"

Her husband sat at the table, overall straps drooping from his thin shoulders. He looked at her with eyes reddened by sun and dust, then wearily rose and followed her to the porch.

The first hint of autumn was in the air, a subtle change in color and texture, a lesser green in the trees, a deepening purple on the distant hills. He listened, and she imagined she saw a fleeting light in his lined face.

"Sounds like a calliope," he said.

She nodded, smiling softly, remembering carnivals and calliopes and carousels. She saw herself, a chubby toddler, secure in her father's arms, high on the back of a magic horse; thought of her own children, scrubbed and rosy, their laughter pure joy in that whirl of light and music.

"Oh Dan, let's go down. Please," she said, grabbing both his hands.

He looked out at the rock-strewn pasture, the orchard, heavy with apples, the garden, vivid with squash and pumpkin and the last of the tomatoes, the fallen trees ready to be sawed and split for firewood. He shook his head. "Can't. Too much work to do."

"But it's Labor Day," she protested.

He grinned, for it was a standing joke between them, the ludicrous notion that no work was to be done on Labor Day. He drew her to him and tucked her head under his chin. Although disappointed and a little miffed, she returned his embrace, and they stood for a moment, fitted together like two spoons in a drawer.

Then he turned and picked up the chain saw and a can of gas. Nellie watched him plod up the rocky hill to the huge oak brought down by a summer storm, not quite believing that he, that they both, had grown old.

Work, work, work and more work. Was that all fifty years on this mountain had gotten them? She knew she was being unreasonable. It was only a merry-go-round, for heaven's sake, a child's ride. But oh, how the children had enjoyed it. She could almost hear their delighted squeals as the horses trotted up and down, round and round, going nowhere.

Some folks, she supposed, would say that of her and Dan. Scratching out a living, just getting by, year after year after year. Going nowhere. *But they would be wrong,* she thought, setting her mouth in a stubborn line. It had been a good life. In spite of it all, it *was* a good life. She was just a silly old women, wasting time, chasing after something that was over and done. Getting all sappy over the memory of her babies on a merry-go-round. Her babies indeed! They were grandparents now, every one of them.

Dan was right. There was work to be done. Labor Day already. So little time before winter. She took a basket from the porch and began to pick the tomatoes, both red and green, pulling and stacking the bare vines as she went. She would can the ripe ones, wrap a few of the best green ones in newspaper and store them in the cellar to ripen. The rest would go into green tomato mincemeat. Dan loved it, and, after all these years, she still got a rush of pleasure in setting a fresh-baked pie, fragrant with spices, before him.

She could hear the tune plainly now, and began to hum along. *Love Makes the World Go Round.* Coming to the end of a row, she stopped to catch her breath, and the music got a good grip on her, held her and refused to let go. Like a sleepwalker, she carried the heavy basket of tomatoes to the porch, and, shading her eyes against the sun, looked for her husband. He was high on the hill now, just a blur of color. But *she* was going to town.

She washed her face and hands at the pump, ran a comb through her hair, and put on a yellowed straw hat. Its flowers, once red, had faded to dull orange, and they bobbed limply as she wrote a hasty note to Dan and tucked the huge vinyl purse under her arm. Walking slowly, planting her stern black shoes in small careful steps, she made her way down the mountain path.

Clusters of pines, tall and green against the blue, blue sky, clung to the decapitated remains of strip-mined slopes, and below, asters and joe-pye and ironweed painted the fields in shades of purple. Chipmunks skittered among the leaves. Birds, anxious to make the most of the season, gossiped in the trees, but she heard only the music, pulling her on, closer and closer to its whirling center.

Both the village and the carnival had seen better days, but the air was heavy with excitement. Children, wound tight with excitement, ran and shouted and cried. Harried parents, trying their best to keep them in tow, knuckled under to their pleas for soda pop and cotton candy, and just one more ride.

It had been a long time since Nellie had been among so many people, so many strange sights and sounds and smells, and never, that she could recall, alone. Nervously she gripped her purse tight against her body, and, fighting the tide, followed the sound of the calliope. When finally she came to its source, she caught her breath and stopped amid the pushing, jostling crowd, the faded flowers on her hat keeping time with the music. The stream separated and flowed around her. The carousel spun before her. Brightly painted horses with jeweled bridles galloped in place. At the hub, red and blue lights blinked off and on, reflecting in the painted eyes, giving them life. They were irresistible. Nellie stepped up to the ticket booth and rummaged in her purse, searching compartment after compartment.

The cashier, a hard-looking blond with heavy eyebrows and a red mouth, drummed her fingers. Finally fishing out a few crumpled bills, Nellie shoved them through the window.

She chose a white horse with pastel flowers woven into its mane and tail, and with some difficulty, and no little loss of modesty, hoisted herself onto its back. Impatient for the ride to begin, she watched children scramble and scrap, watched parents lift frightened toddlers, watched young couples climb aboard the ride.

In the distance, she could see the lights of the Ferris wheel turning, turning, hear the screams as it reached the top of its arc and started back down.

Then, as the calliope played, she closed her eyes and gave herself up to the music and the rhythm of the magic horse. 'Round and around and around they went, and the skein of years began to unwind. She saw the town as it had been, bustling and prosperous, the hills forested, the streams pure. She saw herself as a young mother, a young wife.

The brass pole was smooth and cool in her hands, and she rubbed it lightly, evoking a summer night, a girl in flowered dimity. The girl rode a white horse, and her head spun, not from the motion of the carousel, but for love of the tall young man who stood beside her. Even now, Nellie could feel his breath as he whispered, "I love you so, Nellie. Marry me. Please."

Could it have been so many years ago? How had it all slipped away so quickly?

Too soon, the carousel slowed and stopped. *Oh no, not yet*, she thought. But the ride was over. Her hands, raised to the sudden coolness on her cheeks, came away wet. Then she felt another hand, rough, callused, stroking her face. She opened her eyes, and as the red and blue lights blinked, the young man in her mind became the tall man who stood beside her now.

"Would you do it all over, Nellie? Would you marry me again, knowing how hard it's been?"

"I would, Daniel Jennings," she replied. "I surely would."

The sun was a red dome above the horizon, and mist swirled in the hollows when finally, hand in hand, they left the noise and the lights and the crowds and turned toward home. Halfway up the mountain, stopping to listen, they still heard the music, clear and sweet as a mountain stream.

Blackberry Time

Pa took vacation from his job at the mill
to go blackberry pickin' up on the hill,
on the hill where the berries hung ripe on the cane,
sweetened by sun and soft summer rain.

With shirt buttoned tight at collar and wrist,
a homemade bucket gripped in each fist,
pants tucked in boots 'gainst chigger and snake,
Pa'd be pickin' 'fore I was awake.

Long about noon, he'd come down the hill,
and I'd trot beside him, eating my fill
of berries still warm with the heat of July,
and plenty left over for jelly and pie.

Then, trailed by a hound and purple-mouthed me,
he'd head for the house and a glass of iced tea.
He'd swat Ma's behind, and she'd give him a shove.
I don't recall Pa ever talkin' 'bout love.

But he took vacation down at the mill
to bring us berries from up on the hill.

What I Learned From Kate

The best part of broccoli is the stalk,
stripped down to its crisp sweet heart;
you can make just about anything from zucchini;
super market vegetables are distant cousins
of those grown by your own hands
in your own garden.

A good housewife
washes and reuses Zip-Loc bags,
saves string and wrapping and ribbon,
recycles leftovers in a hearty soup.
Waste not, want not.

That sitting cross-legged on the floor
at the age of eighty is a rare gift,
and gray hair and wrinkles,
brown spotted hands
only disguise the child within.

And this, too, I learned from Kate—
that the unbearable—
the loss of a husband and two sons—
can be borne,
can be borne with grace and dignity.

A Fine Day To Die

Jonetta stood on the porch of the ramshackle farmhouse looking out at the greening fields and the mountains beyond. She could never remember seeing the sky so blue or so clear.

She was tall and broad-shouldered, dressed in jeans, a red plaid flannel shirt and heavy hiking boots. Her dark hair was cut short, and her eyes, black as storm clouds, seemed to see everything but reflect nothing.

"Hey, Claud," she yelled. "Have you heard the weather report today?"

The woman who stepped into the warm September morning frowned. "Don't call me Claud. You know I hate that!"

"So sorry, sister dear. Please, *please*, forgive me!" Jonetta's mouth curved in a mocking grin. "Well . . . did you hear the weather report or not?"

"I can see you're determined to be disagreeable, Jonetta, but I can rise above that. I always do. I did hear the forecast, not five minutes ago." She looked at the sun just clearing the distant mountains, the cloudless sky. "As you can plainly see, it's going to be a fine day."

The woman, whose given name was Claudia, was slight, almost frail, dressed in white, with light brown braids wound around her head. She carried a slim book of poetry, her index finger marking the place she had stopped reading. They were as different as two women could be—so different it would have been difficult for them to live together peaceably in the same neighborhood, much less the same house.

With a saintly smile, the sister generally known as the nice one, the pretty one, held out a string bag. "Here, Jonny, you'll be wanting some lunch."

It was an unaccustomed kindness, and the big woman was touched. "Thanks, Claudie." She hadn't used the affectionate nickname since they were children.

Of course, even then, warm feelings between them were rare. "I swear," their mother would say, "I think you girls fight just for the fun of it. Why can't you get along?" Both women bore scars from those childhood battles, along with some from more recent disputes.

Swinging the heavy backpack to her shoulder as easily as if it were empty, Jonetta stood with one foot cocked up on the step. "I know you like having the house to yourself. I'll be back around noon tomorrow. It'll be cool this evening, so I laid the fire for you. All you have to do is light it." She was surprised to see tears spring to her sister's eyes.

Jonetta strode along the path, across a creek, up into the foothills. Sometimes she had to get away. She just had to. She could take only so much of Claudia and her poems, her *delicate constitution*, and after being cooped up with her all winter, she was long past her limit.

"I do believe the woman fancies herself Emily Dickinson," she muttered. Shedding the backpack against a tree, she dropped down beside it and set her lunch out on a tree stump. She tore off a hunk of the home-baked bread, cut a thick slab of cheese, and thought about yesterday's battle.

That had been a dandy. Baby, Claudia's mangy cat, had shredded Jonetta's favorite jacket. And she gave that sneaky little beast a good kick. Yes, she did, and she wasn't sorry either. "That stupid animal will come up missing someday," Jonetta warned. After all, it was only fair. Her dog disappeared last summer, and she knew in her heart Claudia had something to do with it.

Nevertheless, she was grateful for the lunch, especially the big wedge of blackberry pie and the Thermos of coffee. Hard as it was to find something good to say about ol' Claud, she sure could cook. You had to give her that.

By the time Jonetta finished lunch, a chill wind had sprung up, and clouds scudded across the sun. These mountains were treacherous, especially at this time of year, but she knew that. That's why she had packed her down parka and extra socks, even ski gloves.

She left the path and began climbing. By the time she reached the timberline, black clouds boiled above the horizon, and the temperature was dropping rapidly. She had looked forward to watching the sunset from a favorite rock high on the mountain, but there would be no sunset tonight. Her watch showed just past four, yet it was almost dark and getting colder by the minute.

Pellets of ice and snow whirled around her, stinging her face, blurring her vision. She crawled under a rocky overhang and dropped her pack. Her poncho would serve as a windbreak, and with the sleeping bag and extra clothing, she'd be fine. She would just stay here and wait out the storm.

Jonetta was prepared to spend the night on the mountain, but she was not prepared for what she found when she opened her pack. Her poncho was gone. So were the gloves and extra socks. Her sleeping bag and jacket were there all right—ripped to confetti. A sudden gust of wind blew bits of down into her face like a taunt. The matches were there too, a sodden mass, and the plastic bag of high-energy trail mix held only wood chips and pebbles. And a note, cut from a magazine and pasted together. Its a fINe daY tO DIE!

Surprised, but not yet frightened, Jonetta gave a hoot of laughter. *Claud, Claud, Claud. You always were a liar and a sneak, but you've really outdone yourself this time! So I'll get a little cold, pick up a few scrapes and bruises, might even break a bone or two getting back down the mountain, but die? I don't think so.*

But when she looked out, a curtain had dropped between her and everything else. The snow had become a full-fledged blizzard. She knew! Claudia knew all along! That was the reason for the lunch. She couldn't have Jonetta opening the pack until it was too late.

"This is all your fault, Mother," Jonetta said into the swirling wall of white. She could almost hear the woman saying, *I'll teach you girls to get along if it kills me.* Well. She had certainly given it everything she had while she was alive, and when she died, she left the farm to the sisters jointly, provided they live there together.

The house was big and rambling and in need of repair, but it stood on two hundred acres of the best farmland in Branche County. With the town growing up all around it, it was worth a small fortune.

But as long as both sisters lived, it couldn't be sold. Only if one left—or died—was the other free to do as she chose with the property.

Shivering, Jonetta huddled against the rock at her back, her hands, already numb, shoved into the pack full of shredded fabric and down. She thought of Claudia back at the farm, snug and warm, probably reading her infernal poems aloud. Soon she would be lighting a fire in the fireplace.

Jonetta imagined the flames, crackling, glowing red and orange and yellow, licking the kindling, catching the first log, finally igniting the sticks that were not wood.

Her obsidian eyes glittered, and her lips cracked into a smile. *You're right, as usual, Claudie. It's a fine day to die.*

All Because Of A Shoe

I ran all the way home from school that Monday, my hand curled around the note in my pocket. I had finally gotten a good part in the Thanksgiving play—not just a turkey or a Pilgrim—and couldn't wait to tell Mother and Daddy. But as soon as I turned the corner, I heard the racket. *Uh oh*, I said to myself, *they're at it again*.

Sure enough, when I opened the door, there they were, Mother and Daddy, standing nose to nose, screaming in each other's face. Mother was a little thing, but when she got mad, she seemed to puff up, bigger and bigger, like one of those blow fish at Sea World. Once I heard her tell Aunt Midge that she just blew up about something or other, and every time she and Daddy got into a fight, I was afraid she just might. I imagined bits of Mother flying everywhere, landing on the floor and the furniture like the sparkles that Grandma Galloway always put inside my birthday cards.

They didn't even stop for breath when I came in. No *hello*. No *how was school*. Nothing. I figured that wasn't the best time to tell them about the Thanksgiving program, and me being picked for John Alden and all. About needing a costume, which, I suddenly realized, cost money, which was probably exactly what they were fighting about. It usually was.

I dropped my books in the hall and went to my room, took the note from my pocket and tossed it on the dresser. It wasn't really such a big deal. I already knew what Mother would say anyway. *Well, of course, you got a boy's part, Carla. You're bigger than anybody in your class*. Then she'd laugh that little laugh that said *just kidding*, but I'd know she wasn't. I shut the door and lay down on the bed, the nasty words buzzing around the room like horseflies.

I put my fingers in my ears, but it was no use. Finally I grabbed my jacket and headed for Aunt Martha's.

She was really Daddy's aunt, my great-aunt. She was real old—and *ugly*. Oh my, but she was ugly! Her white hair stuck out every which way, and her mouth—Mother always said it was as tight as a rusted hinge. And mean? Even Daddy said she was the meanest woman God ever put on His good green earth. She looked enough like a witch to scare any kid, and let me tell you, the worst brats in the neighborhood didn't mess with her. Yet, when Mother and Daddy fought, which was pretty often, I couldn't think of anyplace else to go. So, there I was, headed for Aunt Martha's, two blocks up, two blocks over, third house on the left.

When I was little, I thought her house looked like the witch's house in *Hansel and Gretel,* with all those funny little curlicues around the porch, and the bushes growing up past the windows. I sat down on the steps, dreading to go in, too miserable to stay where I was. The concrete was cold and damp through my britches; my fingers were numb, and my nose was beginning to run. I watched big gray clouds race across the sky, over bare branches that clicked and clattered in the wind, and thought about hot chocolate and my fuzzy slippers, and wished . . . Oh, well.

I finally knocked on the door and Aunt Martha opened it without a word. I wasn't welcome there; I knew that. But with the angry words banging against the walls at home, the yelling spilling out onto the sidewalk, where else could I go?

It didn't take me long to warm up in that room. If I had dared, I would have said it was hotter than hell, but I didn't, because I didn't want to go there. I sat on the hard chair in the parlor, the stiff upholstery scratching my bare legs. The curtains were lace, and little crocheted things covered the tables, the chairs, and the big old sofa where Aunt Martha always sat. I watched dust slide down streaks of light to the dark furniture, sneezed as the funny dead smell tickled my nose. I tugged at my hair, picked the scab on my knee.

Aunt Martha just sat there on her sofa crocheting, her eyes over the tops of her glasses never blinking, like the lizards down at the pet store. Her tiny little feet in tiny yellow shoes were planted flat on the floor like two dandelions sprouting from the dirt-colored carpet. My, but she was proud of those feet. So vain she'd walk on her hands if she could, Mother always said. The way I figured it, God gave her those pretty little feet to make up for her being so ugly.

After a while, I got tired of watching the dust settle and slid from the chair. She never blinked, and the crochet hook never stopped as I sneaked into her bedroom, eased the door open and sat there, half in and half out of the closet, counting her shoes. She must have had about a million pairs—every kind, every color you could ever imagine. I never saw her wear the same pair twice.

I jammed my bare feet into first one pair and then another and tiptoed around the bedroom. They pinched. Every time we went shopping, Mother would say, "Carla, you're getting big as a horse. Just like your Daddy." I tried hard to stop growing, but . . . Anyway, Grandpa Galloway didn't think I was big as a horse. He always called me his fine bonny lass. Then one day, he just up and went to heaven.

I was thinking about him, about how much I missed him, when old Satan himself reached out and put temptation right square in front of me. There they were, tucked in the corner of the closet. Pilgrim shoes. John Alden shoes. Shiny black shoes with silver buckles. I looked at my dirty tennies and knew for sure they wouldn't do for John. I fished the shoes out and tried them on. A little tight, but they'd do. Aunt Martha would never miss one pair of shoes; she probably never wore them anyway. I stuffed them down the front of my pants and zipped my jacket over them.

When I peeked around the door, Aunt Martha snapped open the cover of the old-fashioned watch that dangled between her bosoms. (That's what Mother said a lady should call them.)

"It's getting late," she said. "Get out of here. Go on now."

I went. I wondered if she knew what a terrible thing I'd done. I'd broken one of the Thou Shalt Nots. I wished, oh, how I wished, those shoes were back where I found them.

At home, there was no more yelling, no crying. Just the most awful quiet. And in a quiet like that, you don't talk about John Alden, and you sure don't talk about stolen shoes.

Mother finally noticed them, of course. She never missed anything for long.

"Aunt Martha gave them to me," I insisted. "I'm going to be John Alden, and she gave them to me."

Stealing and then lying. That was two Thou Shalt Nots.

I hid them under my bed, practiced my part until I knew it upside down and sideways. I was excited, and yet . . . Oh, I'd done such a bad thing!

When Wednesday night finally came, I was too nervous to eat supper, and my stomach started to growl as our teacher, Miss Halliday, welcomed the parents and told who was doing what. Then, there I was, standing on the stage, the lights shining in my eyes, the cardboard hat on my head, my stomach growling, and the shoes beginning to pinch and burn like hellfire, like all the wickedness in my whole body had settled in my feet. I figured I must be standing in that lake of fire and brimstone that Brother Beamis talked about in revival, and I expected the flames to rise up and consume me at any minute.

"Repent of your sins! Repent, I say!" Brother Beamis would yell, gripping the edge of the pulpit and leaning over so that he was looking right at me. "Call on sweet Jesus to save you, and He will lift you out of that fiery furnace."

I prayed. Oh, how I prayed. "Save me sweet Jesus," I pleaded, just when I was supposed to say my part. "Save me sweet Jesus!" There wasn't a sound for a few seconds, then everyone began to laugh, louder and louder until it seemed the whole world was laughing. At me.

I was ruined, shamed for the rest of my life. But worse than that, I was a sinner—a thief and a liar. I'd never see Grandpa Galloway again. I knew that, because wicked little girls don't go to heaven. How many times had Mother told me that? And Brother Beamis, too.

I hid myself in my room, and the shoes in the farthest corner of the closet. They waited there, black and evil, and I could see them even with the door closed. For days I imagined I could smell something burning. I knew it was a smell I'd better get used to, because I was going to hell. No question about that.

Not long after, Mother and Daddy called me into the den and told me to sit down. From the looks on their faces, I knew this was serious. So . . . they'd found out about the terrible thing I'd done. It would be a relief to get it out in the open and take my punishment. But it wasn't that; it was something worse. Much worse. *They couldn't live together anymore,* they said. *They were getting a divorce. It was nobody's fault,* they said. *Sometimes these things just happen.*

But I knew better. I knew why.

How many times had I heard Brother Beamis talk about death being the wages of sin, and the moaning and gnashing of teeth in the fiery pit? But never—not even once—did he mention the wages of sin *before* you die. Now, I'm not saying that Grandma Galloway's, where we moved after the divorce, was like hell, but it wasn't any picnic either. And I knew why, too. It was because of those shoes, black as sin, buried under a pile of rags in the back of the closet on Baker Street.

Mother got a job as night cook at the Jolly Trolley Diner. When she came home in the mornings, smelling of grease and smoke, I would lean against her, silently begging her to forgive me, but she always pulled away. "For heavens sake, Carla, quit layin' all over me. I'm tired. I had a hard night. Gotta get some sleep. You be quiet now and mind your granny, you hear?"

Between Mother sleeping days and Grandma's nervous condition, I had to be real quiet. All the time. Grandma took in laundry, and her house was always steamy, heavy with the clean smell of Rinso and boiled Argo starch, and the only sound was the schwee schwee schwee of the old wringer washer, or the click clack of Grandma's knitting needles.

The only nice thing was Grandpa Galloway's garden—it was full of flowers with funny names like four-o'clocks and snapdragons and petunias and carnations and zinnias. Grandma Galloway said Grandpa had a green thumb, but it could be she was just teasing, because I never saw it. In the evenings, when I ran through the wet grass catching lightning bugs in a Mason jar, the spicy carnations reminded me of him. I decided the garden was a better way to remember someone than some big old stone in the graveyard.

Many a night I cried myself to sleep. I missed Grandpa so much, and I knew I would never see him again. He was in heaven, and I wouldn't be going *there*. Other nights, I was afraid to go to sleep after praying, *If I should die before I wake*. I didn't want to die, and I especially didn't want to go to hell.

I didn't see much of Daddy after the divorce, and I only saw Aunt Martha once, when I was fifteen, at Grandpa Cooper's funeral. She looked the same. After six years, she still looked exactly the same.

"Do you remember Carla?" Mother said, real loud and slow, pushing me forward.

"Oh yes," Aunt Martha said, eyeing my size nines. "I remember her."

She knew. I knew she knew.

And now, all these years later, I look out the window and watch my kids playing—Caitlyn a sturdy blond three-year-old, and Billy, just past five, wiry and dark like his daddy. In my lap is a small package wrapped in yellowed tissue, and in my hand a note from Daddy. *Aunt Martha died last week*, he says. *She wanted you to have this.* That's all. No *How are you?* No *How are the kids?* No *Love, Dad.* My fingers worry the ragged edge of the paper as I think about the shoes and the divorce and all that happened after. That was a long time ago, I tell myself. Water under the bridge, and yet . . .

The shoes had nothing to do with it; I *know* that. It wasn't my fault. I know that, too. Still, I have to wonder if divorce is hereditary. I'm afraid it's just a matter of time before Bill and I call our kids into the den and tell them the same lies my parents told me. We've always fought like cats and dogs, right from the beginning, but it got worse when Caitlyn was born eight weeks early, and the hospital and doctor bills just kept coming. It was a bad time. He said things. I said things. And one thing led to another. Now, neither of us says much.

Finally, I pick up the package. The paper crumbles in my fingers, and the dry dead smell brings those miserable afternoons at Aunt Martha's crashing down around me. I open the small box, and there lies the half-remembered pendant watch with a tag attached. In what I suppose to be Aunt Martha's handwriting, lacy and old fashioned, is the message: *For Carla. Tell her I forgive her.*

She forgives me? I open the cover and look at the yellowed face. The hands, tarnished, stand at 10:22, and I wonder how many days or months or years Aunt Martha's forgiveness has lain hidden away in some dark drawer. I wonder how long I carried the weight of my childish crime after the pardon had already been granted. So she forgave me. Does it matter? Does it change anything?

I slip the chain over my head and feel the weight of the pendant between my breasts. *Whatever happened to those damned shoes,* I wonder. Are they still stuffed in the back of that closet? Is the house even still there?

Then, remembering my nine-year-old self standing on that stage, terrified, in paper hat and hot shoes, shouting "Save me, sweet Jesus," at the astonished audience, I begin to laugh. I laugh until I'm weak, until my stomach hurts and tears run down my face. I take the pendant off, heft its weight in my hand, then drop it back into the box.

I'm still mopping my eyes with the back of my hand when I step onto the porch.

Billy runs to me. "Mommy, why are you crying?"

"I'm not crying, honey. I just thought of something that happened a long time ago, and it seemed kinda funny."

I hug him hard and gather Caitlyn in with my other arm. "You kids come on in and get washed up for supper. Daddy will be home soon."

Photo Credits

Wrinkled Woman Profile©RazvanPhotography, Radu Razvan, Cluj Napoca, Transylvania, Romania, www.razvanphotostock.com
Weeds Overgrown©Gary Andrews, Northamptonshire, United kingdom
Winter Night©Andrey Tetyushev, Ukraine
Window Pane©Perry Correll, United States
Grandfather1©John Wollwerth, Beaufort, United States, Wollwerth Imagery, wollwerthimagery.com
Autumn©Rui Vale de Sousa, Guimaraes, www.ruivaledesousa.com
Wedding Boquet©Alena Ozerova, Ukraine
Summer Creek©Victoria Smith, United States
Heaven©Mike Amerson, Henderson, United States
Mountain Valley©Radoslav Stoilov, Bulgaria
Hope©Jessica Bethke, De Forest, United States
Crossword Puzzel©Adrian Hughes, United Kingdom
Porch Swing©Ardith Shishmian, United States
Ornament©Emilia Kun, Canada
Heron©Paul Yates, North Vancouver, Canada
Autumn Leaves©John Gavin, London, United Kingdom
Flying Birds©Elena Elisseeva, Toronto, Canada, www.elenaphoto.com
Colorful Primroses©Katharine Wittfeld, Germany
Pretty Beam©Lori LeBlanc, Friendswood, United States www.digitallifephotos.com
Urban Scene©Dan Ionut Popescru, Romania
Vintage Book©Makwym Yemelyanov, Ukraine
Blackberry©Gennadij Nikolaewitch Kurilin, Moskow, Russia

Acknowledgments

This book would not have been possible without the support, patience and encouragement of my husband, Stanley.

To the many friends and relatives—my cheerleaders—who have always been there for me, what can I say? Thank you seems so inadequate.

A special thanks to all my writer/editor friends, especially Wilma Acree and Sandy Tritt. They have held my hand, patiently and gently corrected my errors, even lied a little when I was discouraged. They have not only encouraged me to go where I would not have dared go alone; they have accompanied me.

Thanks also to the West Virginia Commission on the Arts for the 2007 Fellowship in Literature, which helped make this book possible, and to the editors and staff of the following anthologies, journals and periodicals who have paid me the ultimate compliment in choosing my work for publication.

Best of West Virginia Writers—	Gardens
Confluence—	Cousin Joyce's Second Wedding
	A Fine Day to Die
	The Waiting Room
First for Women—	Small Shadows, Silent Dreams
Grab-a-Nickel—	After Supper
	Aphasia
	Offerings
	Second Chances
Grit—	Blackberry Time
Mountain Voices—	Like a Gift
	Second Chances
Weeping with Those Who Weep—	Permission to Leave
Wild Sweet Notes II—	After Supper
	Blackberry Time
	Offerings
Woman's World—	Like a Gift

About the Author

Patsy Evans Pittman's stories and poems were first published in a children's weekly while she was still in elementary school. Her next publication, however, did not occur until many years later, after a thirty-year career with GMAC.

Since then, her short stories and poems, many of which are included in this collection, have been published in *FIRST for Women, Woman's World* and *Grit*, among others, as well as in several anthologies. Her non-fiction has appeared in *Guideposts Books, Cup of Comfort, Ideals, Country Woman,* and others.

She has won numerous awards from *Writers Digest,* West Virginia Writers, Midwest Writers, Alabama Writers Conclave and Barbour County Workshop, and received a 2007 Fellowship in Literature from the West Virginia Commission on the Arts.

Mrs. Pittman and her husband Stanley live in Vienna, West Virginia, within a few miles of her birthplace. Between them, they have six children and fourteen grandchildren.

"I have no desire to write the great American novel," she says. "It is poems and short stories, lovingly crafted, word after word after word, that break my heart, gladden my soul and keep me awake nights. And when I see one of my creations in print—ahhh, it doesn't get any better than that."

Photo by Olan Mills